"They Tell Me You're Trouble,"

Matt Harrigan said.

Chyna met his gaze head on. "That depends," she said tersely, "on your definition of trouble."

"My definition of trouble, Miss O'Brien, is someone who disrupts production, who makes waves in a calm sea." There was no mistaking the warning in his voice.

"If the sea is calm," Chyna said, a slight smile on her lips, "there will be no waves. I promise."

"I'm surprised they hired you, what with your reputation."

"I'm not," she replied challengingly. "I'm the best there is." As Matt Harrigan was soon to find out!

MARIE NICOLE

is a natural romance writer because her own life has been so romantic. She met her husband-to-be in tenth grade and began dating him in college. The first time he kissed her he made the room fade away, and things have only gotten better for them since.

Dear Reader:

SILHOUETTE DESIRE is an exciting new line of contemporary romances from Silhouette Books. During the past year, many Silhouette readers have written in telling us what other types of stories they'd like to read from Silhouette, and we've kept these comments and suggestions in mind in developing SILHOUETTE DESIRE.

DESIREs feature all of the elements you like to see in a romance, plus a more sensual, provocative story. So if you want to experience all the excitement, passion and joy of falling in love, then SILHOUETTE DESIRE is for you.

For more details write to:

Jane Nicholls
Silhouette Books
PO Box 236
Thornton Road
Croydon
Surrey CR9 3RU

MARIE NICOLE
A Woman
Of Integrity

Silhouette Desire
Originally Published by Silhouette Books
division of
Harlequin Enterprises Ltd.

First published in Great Britain 1985
by Mills & Boon Ltd, 15–16 Brook's Mews, London W1A 1DR

© Marie Nicole 1985

Silhouette, Silhouette Desire and Colophon are Trade Marks of Harlequin Enterprises B.V.

ISBN 0 373 05197 2

22–0985

Made and printed in Great Britain by
Richard Clay (The Chaucer Press) Ltd,
Bungay, Suffolk

This book is dedicated to
Jessica.
May she grow up to be
a woman of integrity.
(But not a stuntwoman.
My heart couldn't take it.)

1

They tell me you're trouble," Matt Harrigan said with an edge to his deep voice.

"That depends," Chyna O'Brien responded tersely, looking up and meeting his gaze head on.

"On what?"

"On your definition of trouble."

The two stood scrutinizing one another the way the Indians and Columbus might have at their first fateful meeting in the New World. Each was filled with curiosity and apprehension. Neither knew what to expect.

Chyna waited for the producer's next words. For a moment she forgot how uncomfortable she was, broiling beneath the intense Philippine sun that was beating down on her and the other people involved in setting up the location shots for Bounty Studios' latest film. Her china blue eyes stared up unwaveringly at the stern, uncompromising face of the producer. She hadn't expected to be accosted so soon. She had only been in Manila three hours.

"My definition of trouble, Miss O'Brien—"

"*Mrs.* O'Brien," she corrected. Neil might be gone, but she had still been his wife, she thought.

"My definition of trouble, *Mrs.* O'Brien," Matt said, beginning again, "is someone who disrupts production, who makes waves in a calm sea." There was no mistaking the warning in his voice.

"If the sea is calm," Chyna said, a slight smile on her lips, "there'll be no waves." She could see the skepticism in his eyes. "I promise."

His dark brows knitted in a scowl. "I'm surprised the stunt coordinator hired you," he told her flatly, eyeing her diminutive, well-proportioned figure with no visible reaction. He was the type, Chyna decided, who let nothing get in the way of business.

"I'm not," she replied, jutting out her delicately shaped chin. She reminded him of a bantam rooster.

"Oh?" he challenged. For a moment she thought she detected just a hint of interest in his green eyes.

"I'm the best there is," she informed him. It wasn't a matter of boasting. It was a matter of record.

"Are you, now?" he asked. She thought she heard the faintest touch of amusement in his voice.

"Yes," she answered firmly. "I was trained by the best—until some director's overzealous desire to cut corners cost him his life."

She could tell by the look on his face that Matt didn't like the turn the conversation was taking. All around them, people were passing by, occupied with their own separate personal tasks. Neither Chyna nor Matt took any notice of the crowd as they eyed one another, two boxers coming out of their corners to

8

touch gloves before the first bell sounded. The tension hung heavily in the humid air.

Just then someone called Matt's name and he turned his dark blond head away from her. The bright sun accented his profile as Chyna took in the rugged planes of his tanned face, her eyes skimming along the almost perfect cheekbones. He was the image of a proud man. His nose, she caught herself thinking, might have been a little smaller. It marred the otherwise classical lines of his face. But it did add a dimension of reality.

After nodding toward the man who stood beckoning to him, Matt momentarily turned his attention back to Chyna. "No waves," he warned her, his eyes clouding just a little.

"It's a large ocean—the waves go in both directions," Chyna pointed out as Matt began to walk away. She could tell by the set of his shoulders that he didn't like her answer.

Despite her outer bravado, Chyna was as surprised as Matt was that she had been hired. It had been less than a year since she had raised her voice against the studio's flagrant disregard for life and limb. After Neil's death she had been instrumental in organizing the Committee for Safety Precautions, and had tried in vain to get the heads of the larger studios to lend a sympathetic ear—or any ear at all—to the problems the stunt crew faced.

Sighing, Chyna picked up her canvas bag and slung it over her shoulder. On the flight over here, ever the optimist, she had hoped for a fresh start. All she had wanted to do was concentrate on getting her timing right for the dangerous stunts that lay ahead of her. But that was before she had learned that Matt Harrigan was the producer of *The Adventurer,* and that he would be coming along to oversee the entire production.

Chyna pressed her lips together. Harrigan had been the producer on Neil's last film. In the beginning she had held him partially responsible for Neil's death, even though he hadn't even been on the set. Word had it that the director had been rushing in order to satisfy a front office edict from Harrigan. She had never met him, but she had spent several months damning his soul. A year had given her a long time to think. She had ceased blaming the man logically. But emotionally was another story.

Now he was here.

And instead of telling him about the feelings she had harbored, she was going to have to bite her lip and behave. It was either that or get out of the business. This was her first real assignment since Neil's death. If she was thrown off this picture, her career was over. What a rotten predicament, she thought miserably, slapping away a hungry mosquito. This was definitely going to be an endurance test.

"Hey, Chyna, over here!"

Chyna turned quickly. Her chestnut hair, heavy with the weight of absorbed humidity, didn't respond to the motion and blocked her view. She sighed. It was going to be a long two months. But at least she was working again, she reminded herself.

"Hi, Pepper," Chyna said, smiling as she tucked a strand of wayward hair behind her ear.

The long-legged stuntwoman strode toward Chyna eagerly. Her dutchboy haircut, also a victim of the humidity, hung about her face. Her white shorts and tube top were already stained with perspiration. "What are you doing here?" she asked excitedly.

"Rolf twisted some arms and landed a few gags for me," Chyna answered modestly. She remembered the first time Neil had used the term and she had corrected him, thinking he had meant to say "gig." That had been before he had drawn her so completely into the world of stuntwork.

"So they actually hired you!" Pepper said, surprised.

"They better have," Chyna answered with a laugh. "I don't fall out of planes for free."

"Saw you talking to that hunk. How did you get to first base with him so fast?"

"That 'hunk' is the producer," Chyna informed her. "And I wasn't on first base. I was in the dugout, being given a warning about messing up the game plan." She looked over the taller woman's shoulder in the general direction that Matt had taken. He was busy talking to several grips who were moving sound equipment.

Was it just her imagination, or was he looking her way? What was he afraid she was going to do, organize everyone into a strike five minutes after she got here? Was she going to be looking over her shoulder the entire time she was here? The thought brought a frown to her face.

"What's the matter?" Pepper asked.

Chyna shook her head. "Nothing. Look, let's move. I think I'm getting deep fried."

Pepper followed her to the dubious shade cast by the long, wispy leaves of an exotic tree in the throes of shedding its bark.

"I'm still surprised to see you," Pepper said. "I thought that after Neil died and they gave you such a rough deal, you'd kind of, you know, disappear from the movie scene. . . ."

Chyna smiled at the notion. No, she wasn't the disappearing type. She was a survivor, a hanger-on no matter what. Her marriage to Neil had just reinforced that. Neil. Gentle, soft-spoken, competent Neil, who had been so good at his work, so careful. If he hadn't allowed that director to hurry him that day, if he had only checked the airbag himself instead of taking the stunt coordinator's word for it . . .

"What?" Chyna suddenly realized that Pepper had asked her a question and was waiting for an answer.

"Where are you staying?" the woman repeated.

"Same place you are, I guess," Chyna answered, thinking of the wooden two-by-four shacks she had seen lining the road a quarter of a mile back. From all appearances, they'd need considerable upgrading just to be called cabins. The studio didn't go to any trouble for the lesser people involved in making a movie. Only the stars and the brass rated accommodations that ran the range from tolerable to terrific, depending on how much pull each person exerted. Chyna had no doubts that Matt's personal trailer was the last word in comfort.

Pepper screwed up her mobile face as she slung her unwieldy suitcase over her shoulder. "Think there'll be bugs?" she asked.

"I'm only hoping the bugs leave a little space for us," Chyna replied philosophically. "They might resent us invading their territory." Together they began to head back in the direction of the shacks.

"I can't see why they couldn't film this thing in

Hawaii. They've got palm trees there, too," Pepper complained.

"Would be nice, wouldn't it?" Chyna slapped away still another large mosquito that threatened to deplete her blood supply. "But I think they need more in the way of scenery than just the palm trees. The movie is supposed to take place somewhere in the Philippines in the 1930s—so what better place to film it than here? This certainly fills the bill," Chyna said, gesturing with her free hand at the lush area.

"Not my bill," Pepper muttered.

Chyna laughed in agreement as they approached their living quarters.

The sunbleached shack they decided on was plopped down between two lanky palm trees which stood like two drunken centurian guards with choppy, unkempt haircuts. It was a tiny shack. Tiny, Chyna thought, as in "crammed," not as in "cute."

Pepper hung back, as if expecting Chyna to do battle with any stray tropical insects or rodents that had staked out the shack first. Chyna couldn't understand how anyone who didn't mind risking her life daily could be afraid of a mouse.

As she pushed the creaky door closed behind them, Chyna felt the prick of a splinter entering her palm. She glanced down at the sliver. Was this an omen of things to come? she wondered dryly. Wasn't having to work on one of Matt Harrigan's pictures enough?

The light that made its way through the dirty, cracked windowpane was just bright enough to highlight the primitiveness of the living facilities.

"Ugh," Pepper moaned, for once justified in her complaint, Chyna thought.

"Look," Chyna announced brightly, "indoor

13

plumbing." After sweeping away a sticky, grayish web that appeared to have been part of the rusty pump handle since time immemorial, Chyna began working the handle gingerly, afraid that it might come off in her hand. To her surprise the first thing to emerge from the antiquated faucet was an unwilling, multilegged hairy creature.

Finally, through her diligent efforts, Chyna produced a slow drip. She tried to convert it into something resembling running water, but she might as well have been trying to turn water into wine. Several additional minutes of hard pumping yielded nothing but a cramp in her upper forearm.

"We'll work on it," she promised Pepper, who looked far from optimistic.

The only furniture in the room consisted of two old, rickety cots.

"Well, at least we won't have to sleep on the floor," Chyna commented.

"How long did they say we're going to be here?" Pepper asked.

"Two months," Chyna said.

The atmosphere in the shack felt oppressive. The air hung there, thick and sticky. Chyna pushed aside a curtain which had worn so thin that it came apart in her hand. Sighing, she tossed it on the wooden floor as she tried to pry open the window. It wouldn't budge, and she gave up.

"Two months," Pepper echoed unhappily, sinking down on her cot. It groaned as it accepted her weight.

Chyna knew how she felt. But stuntpeople couldn't afford to be choosy. You never knew when the next job was coming, and if you turned one down, there were more than enough people out there willing to take your place, even if they were ill prepared to do so. That's when accidents happened. Then, and when you had thoughtless people in charge. Chyna's mind went back to Matt. Rolf hadn't told her that Harrigan would ultimately be in charge of the picture.

A faint smile came to her lips. He had probably thought she wouldn't take the job if she had known. And she probably wouldn't have. But she was here now, and she would have to make the best of it. She tried to bury the angry feelings simmering just below the surface of her mind.

"Hey," Pepper said, breaking into Chyna's moody thoughts, "I'm starved. When's our next meal? I haven't eaten since I landed."

"Whenever they set up the cafeteria, I guess."

"Well, let's go see," the other woman urged.

Chyna looked at her unpacked bag and decided that it would keep. After pushing the bag under her bed, she followed Pepper out the door, not bothering to try to lock it on her way out. She was sure that neither the lock nor the door would be strong enough to keep anyone out.

Other people must have been of the same mind as Pepper, Chyna decided, because parts of the kitchen were already set up. A handful of the production staff were there ahead of them, filling their trays. Most of them were just getting something to drink, she noticed. Overhead the sun hung like a big ball of fire, letting no one below forget its hard, merciless presence for a moment. Chyna picked up a tall glass of lukewarm iced tea, bypassing a ham and cheese on rye that looked as if it too yearned for cooler temperatures.

She and Pepper sat down beneath a tree, trying to

keep out of the way of the cables being strung from monstrous-looking generators. The clanging of hammers was just beginning to be heard. The crew were setting up the facades necessary for some of the outdoor scenes. Chyna didn't envy them their task. It felt too hot to talk, much less work. She leaned against the tree, watching the scene that was haphazardly unfolding all around her.

She loved this life, loved being a part of the seamless world of make-believe that was somehow pieced together from a thousand miscellaneous loose ends. She knew that when she became immersed in her part of all this, all her thoughts, all her other problems, would slip somewhere far away—almost as if they had never existed at all.

Several stuntmen drifted by to exchange a few pleasantries. Everyone was surprised to see Chyna in their midst again.

"Wonderful to see you!" one stuntman enthused. "I didn't think you'd be back working so soon."

Soon?

To other people soon meant that their own lives had gone on as planned; they never noticed that time had been passing unfruitfully by for someone else. "Soon" had been a year for Chyna, a long, endless, creeping year that had been full of gnawing emptiness. It had started with an emotional earthquake: Neil's death. It had limped on its way as she helped form the committee that tried to have rules passed and adhered to by the boards of all the studios. And it had ground to a halt as both she and her rules were rejected. Oh, there had been a token investigation into Neil's death, and everyone, including Matt, had been absolved of blame. The director had received a wrist-slapping and a five hundred dollar fine. Five hundred dollars in exchange for Neil's life. No charges. He had died for nothing.

And the work offers for Chyna had ceased. There had been little or nothing she could do except wait and hope things would change. In the meantime, she took odd jobs. Rolf, a friend and fellow stuntman, came through, giving her a job with his stunt workshop more out of kindness than out of any necessity for extra help. Eventually, using his influence and her reputation as one of the best stuntwomen in the field, Rolf had talked Alex, the head stunt coordinator, into giving her a chance on this film.

But why did it have to be on *his* picture? Thinking of Matt, Chyna found herself looking for him. It was hard to miss the man. Although he wasn't overly tall, close to six feet at most, he managed to stand out, a center of calm within the storm of moving bodies. The first day on the set was always marked by spurts of furious energy alternated with long periods of inactivity. No one was sure what they were doing most of the time, and everyone looked to someone else for instructions. When that someone turned up, issuing orders, a frenzied pace would ensue for a while and then subside once again.

It was unusual to have the producer on the set, Chyna thought, especially when the film was being made on location. Normally, when producers came at all, they came for a short visit. Harrigan appeared to be settling in for the duration. Chyna had heard that Harrigan, always a stickler for detail, had become even more personally involved in his projects after Neil's accident. She wondered if he was doing it out of guilt.

She watched him now. He appeared to be a portrait of subdued control, his manner a definite contrast to the director's. The latter kept gesticulating, pointing to people and things as if, in his mind, they were all lumped together. He was shorter than Matt and wore a gaily knotted neckerchief which for some reason wasn't wilting, and he looked like a caricature of a high-ranking enemy general from an old war movie. His bald head added to the demonic picture that he seemed to delight in casting.

But it wasn't the director who held Chyna's attention. Her eyes kept drifting back to Matt, even as different people vied for her attention with their greetings.

Annoyed. That was the word for it, she decided. Underneath his control there was an underlying layer of annoyance. Was she the cause of it? she wondered. She had seen firsthand his displeasure when he had discovered that the stunt coordinator had hired her.

Well, no matter, she thought as his powerful, athletic figure cut across her line of vision once again. She had other things to think about.

She rose, dusting off her faded jeans. They were adhering to her legs and making her decidedly uncomfortable. She was going to go and change into shorts. When she raised her eyes she noticed that her movements had caught Matt's attention. He was watching her again. She was used to people watching her. That was her job, to do things that made them sit up and take notice. But this was different. There was something about the way Matt watched her that made her uneasy. He was probably trying to psych her out, she told herself, and get her to quit the picture. Her presence was too much of a reminder of the fact that his schedule had cost a man his life. Well, if he thought he was going to get rid of her that easily, he was mistaken. She was here for the duration, and nothing and no one was going to make her leave.

"C'mon," she said to Pepper, who was talking to a member of the crew. "Let's go and find Alex and let him know we're here," she urged.

"He was watching you," Pepper said in a loud whisper.

"I know," Chyna muttered, instinctively knowing who Pepper was talking about. She left and quickly snaked her way through the construction crew. The more distance she put between herself and Matt Harrigan, the better.

"Hey, where are you rushing to?" Pepper wanted to know as soon as she caught up.

Chyna stopped dead in her tracks. Why *was* she rushing? she asked herself. The stunt coordinator wasn't going anywhere. None of them were. Was she subconsciously trying to avoid being around Matt? She had nothing to hide, nothing to be ashamed of.

"Are you looking for someone?" Matt asked her over the din of the crowd.

Chyna stood perfectly still as he made his way over to her, adrenaline rushing double-time through her veins.

"Hi, I'm Pepper," the blond woman said cheerfully when he reached them.

Matt nodded politely, but it was obvious that he wasn't taking any particular notice of the other woman. His smoky green eyes burned into Chyna's skin, causing more of a reaction than the hot sun. A warm nervousness was creeping over her, and the back of her neck prickled. Either she was in the beginning stages of malaria, or Matt Harrigan was having a definite effect on her. What did that tanned face look like when it was smiling?

Chyna suddenly realized that he had asked her a question and was now waiting for an answer.

"I'm looking for Alex, the stunt coordinator," she said, her throat dry.

"Good," he said solemnly. Chyna could feel herself growing indignant. What did he mean, "good"? Did he think she needed a keeper? "Alex is over there," he said, pointing out a dark-haired man in a sweat-soaked shirt.

Chyna looked in the direction he indicated, and when she turned back to Matt, she found that he was gone.

2

After spending the night on her cot, Chyna began to eye the floor more favorably. At least, she thought as she stretched, trying to reach the sore spot in the center of her back, the floor didn't sink down in the middle.

"Boy," she muttered, feeling more dead than alive, "my neck feels like it's made out of wood."

She received a "mfph" in reply from the almost circular heap in the next cot.

"She could probably sleep through the Apocalypse," Chyna said to the scurrying spider that ambled across her bare foot as she tried to come around.

A shower would be heavenly. But she knew that, as of last night, the shower facilities hadn't been set up yet. Yesterday's sweat felt as if it had settled into a permanent gritty layer on her body.

Oh, well, things wouldn't get any better if she complained, she thought, taking off her pajamas.

Quickly she put on a pair of dark blue shorts and a powder blue halter top. At least she felt a little cooler now, she tried to console herself.

It took her five minutes to get enough water into the basin she had purloined from the prop man to wash her face. She had just finished brushing her teeth when an unidentifiable green bug decided to commit suicide in her water.

"So long, fella," Chyna muttered, dumping the sudsy water into the sink.

Looking over her shoulder, Chyna could see that Pepper had changed position on the cot; two limbs now dangled over the side.

"Want to get a little exercise?" Chyna asked the lump brightly.

"Zoomifh," came the muffled answer.

"I take it," Chyna said wryly, putting a clip in her hair as she raised it off her neck, "that means no."

In response Pepper waved an arm at her, putting off any further conversation. Chyna slipped on her size five running shoes and went out.

She had to blink twice to acclimate her eyes to the brighter light. She hadn't realized how gloomy everything looked inside the shack. Out here there was life, in living color, she mused, taking in the lush foliage.

At this hour of the morning it was too early for most people to be out, so for the moment it felt like a secluded paradise—even if it had to be shared with mosquitoes that were outfitted with bayonets instead of stingers, she thought as she ducked one.

She looked up at the clouds that were moving languidly above her, wisps of cotton across the sky, and a feeling of peacefulness came over her.

Where to run? she pondered—and not get lost. She

didn't quite trust her homing instincts just yet, so she decided that the best place to jog would be along the shoreline of the nearby beach. At least there she wouldn't run the risk of tripping over half-hidden roots. With that settled, she trudged out across the sand.

Just me and the waves, she told herself, listening to the rhythmic slapping of the water against the endless beach. Knowing that running on the wet sand would be good for her leg muscles, Chyna took off her jogging shoes and stuffed her socks into the toes, leaving them on the beach. Warm sand squished between her toes as she paced herself. Soon she fell into a comfortable breathing pattern. She felt as if she could run along the golden beach all day.

Effortlessly she ran along the shoreline, then turned around and started to run back to where she had left her shoes. She began to feel the emotional surge that came from jogging, that inner glow of health and satisfaction with one's own efforts. Time melted away as she relished the euphoric feeling. It wasn't until she was practically on top of him that she realized she was no longer alone. A man in light clothes sat on the beach not far from her shoes.

Matt Harrigan.

She felt her breath growing shorter. As she drew closer Chyna saw that Matt did not appear to be taking any notice of her presence. He sat facing the ocean, looking utterly lost in thought.

Chyna took a deep breath. If she ignored him, she would be being purposely rude, and it would serve no purpose. After all, he *was* the producer. "Hi," she ventured, coming to a halt beside him.

"Shh." He waved a dismissing hand at her.

She could feel her temper rising. She was a person, not a mosquito. "What?"

"I'm thinking," he growled.

"About what?" she said, bending down to retrieve her shoes. "How to cut corners and save time?" she asked. The words had just tumbled out. She couldn't help herself.

He turned his brilliant green eyes on her. "As a matter of fact, yes," he said coolly. "Times are tight. You save wherever and whatever you can."

"Does that include lives?" she asked archly. The words were out of her mouth before she even knew she had thought them.

Matt raised one dark brow—incredibly dark for someone with such fair hair, she thought. "That includes everything," he said firmly.

"I'm glad to hear that," she said evenly. She turned to go, her shoes dangling from her fingertips.

Matt grabbed her wrist, making her drop her shoes. "Are you implying something?" he asked testily.

"If the shoe fits . . ." she said, glancing down at the sand. Why was she harping on this? She knew she didn't really blame Matt anymore. And yet, there were all those deep-seated feelings that she had tried to conquer, those feelings that had kept her awake at night, wondering why Neil had had to die. She had to get them out in the open.

"The shoe doesn't fit," he told her. He drew a deep breath. "I'm sorry about what happened to your husband. I thought my note explained my position."

She looked at him sharply. "What note?"

His expression became slightly puzzled. "The one I sent after the accident. The one you never answered."

"I never answered it because I never got one." Was

he telling the truth? His silence at the time had convinced Chyna of Matt's guilt in the matter. Was he now just making up a convenient lie to smooth things out for the duration of the movie?

For a moment they stared at one another, at an impasse. And then Matt picked up her shoes and handed them to her. When he raised his head, his eyes were level with her breasts. It seemed to Chyna that he was taking his time in straightening up.

"Here."

"Thank you," she said crisply, hiding her embarrassment at his intent stare. "Fine pastime for a grown man," she mumbled. "Staring down the fronts of women's shirts."

"There are worse ways to spend one's time," Matt replied. "Like prejudging people," he added.

Chyna bristled visibly. "I wouldn't be throwing any stones if I were you. You were the one who hauled me aside to give me that thinly veiled warning. What are you afraid I'm going to do, call a strike?" she demanded.

"You seem to be capable of a lot of stupid things—"

"Stupid!" Chyna's voice went up an indignant octave.

He looked unruffled by her tone. "Bringing suit against the studio and trying to get it shut down was a stupid thing to do," he said honestly.

"So is wasting lives," she retorted. "My husband was one of the best in the field. He worked hard and did everything that was expected of him—and then some. He wound up taking a two-hundred-foot dive into an airbag that burst because the director was in too damn much of a hurry to let him check his own equipment. He had a schedule to meet." Chyna's voice dropped slightly. "All Neil's cooperation earned him was a short paragraph on page thirty-nine of the local paper. He was a good, decent, kind man, and he ended up as filler in a tabloid." There was no hiding the bitterness in her voice. Neil had deserved better, much better. More than that, Neil had deserved to live a long, full life and wind up like Rolf, teaching other stuntpeople how to practice their craft safely. Chyna bit her lip. She was showing him more emotion than she had intended. But the pain had been locked in her heart for too long.

"Well, you certainly weren't filler," Matt commented. "You were page one material."

Chyna shrugged, looking off at the sky that was turning a deeper shade of blue. "I wasn't looking for page one. I was looking for something meaningful to come out of his death. I was trying to keep something like that from happening again. Too many stunt-people's lives are cut short by speed," she told him firmly.

Matt looked puzzled. "Drugs?"

"No," she said evenly. "Careless directors hurrying to meet unrealistic production schedules."

Matt studied her for a moment, the slight vein in his temple more prominent than it had been a moment ago. "Shutting down a studio deprives a lot of people of their livelihoods."

Chyna's face was solemn as she met his steady gaze. "At least they would still come home at night."

"Nobody forces stuntmen into that line of work," he pointed out.

She felt her temper growing short and tried vainly to hold on to it. You weren't supposed to shout at your producer. Not if you wanted to go on earning a living in the film business. "That's the kind of argument they used a hundred years ago to justify putting little boys to work in the mines. Nobody forced *them* to go, either."

"This is a little different."

"Is it?" she persisted.

They stood eyeing one another. And then Chyna thought she detected the makings of a smile edge its way onto his rugged face. It was like the sun coming out after a cloudy day. Despite the subject of their discussion, she found herself responding to him before she knew what was happening.

It had been far easier to hold Matt Harrigan responsible when she didn't know what he looked like, when he was just a name in the newspaper. Standing toe to toe with the man was something else again. It wasn't that she was intimidated. She was . . . She didn't quite know what she was.

Looking at him covertly, Chyna was too aware of the taut, hard muscular frame beneath his form-fitting pullover. His shoulders and arms were well developed without a muscle-bound appearance. Since he was wearing shorts, Chyna could see that his muscular development didn't begin and end above the waist. His every movement was filled with sensual grace. He looked more like the star of one of his movies than the producer.

"A fine pastime for a grown woman," she heard him say and realized that she was staring at his V-neckline, taking in the fine layer of evenly distributed hair on his chest.

A red stain worked its way up from her damp neck until it settled on her cheeks. Chyna felt every painful inch of its travels.

"Tit for tat," she retorted without thinking. The red stain turned crimson as Matt threw back his sandy head and laughed out loud. It was a deep, rich, wonderful laugh that she would have enjoyed under different circumstances.

In desperation Chyna looked at her watch. "I've got to get back."

To her utter surprise, rather than nodding dismissively at her, Matt took her arm. Even in her frustrated embarrassment, she felt a definite wave of electricity telegraph itself all through her nervous system.

"I'll walk you back," he offered.

"No, I can find my own way, thank you," she told him. "Besides, I don't want to intrude any more on your precious time." She punctuated her statement with an unreadable smile.

As she forged straight into the forest without so much as a backward glance, Chyna was nonetheless quite aware of the fact that Matt was watching her. She could *feel* it. Her stomach made a noise that was a cross between a rumble and a gurgle, informing her that she had other things to think about besides a pensive, enigmatic producer.

But she couldn't seem to erase Matt's face from her mind. A fine way for you to act, she told herself sternly. What would Neil think about your reactions? *All* your reactions.

Neil would undoubtedly have said forgive and forget. He had been the most mild-mannered man she had ever known. Very different from the way Matt appeared to be. There was a smoldering intensity about Matt that was intriguing.

Intriguing, huh?

"No, no, no! How have you reached your age

without learning the proper way to hold a woman in your arms?"

The words—and their angry tone—cut through Chyna's thoughts as she walked into a clearing and saw the director gesticulating madly. Even from where she was standing, Chyna could see the leading man frowning down at the director's gleaming bald head.

"This way!" Phillip Dussault insisted, taking the leading lady, Sally Kittridge, into his arms and holding her as if she were a vessel of precious wine. "With reverence, not like she's a hamburger from one of those fast food places!" he declared, still not letting go of Sally. "We're shooting a picture about an aristocratic woman, not some flophouse floozie who can be had for a drink!"

"Nobody ever complained about the way I held her before," Evan Beaumont growled.

"That," Dussault said imperiously, "is because you've probably only held flophouse floozies in your arms and worked with tasteless directors. *I* am an artist!" Abruptly he released Sally. "Now let's go, people! Time is money; time is money!" He clapped his hands together impatiently. "Cameras!" he commanded.

Chyna shook her head and kept walking, her stomach leading the way to the cafeteria. There were going to be a lot of arguments and battered egos in the days ahead. She had been on enough sets to know the signs. Well, none of that concerned her. All she wanted was to do her job, collect her pay and go home none the worse for wear.

She got in line behind an actor dressed as a fighter pilot. He wore a natty-looking leather jacket and an old-fashioned cap with earflaps dangling about his thin face. Probably a starstruck extra, she judged. Why else would he be wearing his full costume in the rising heat? she thought, amused.

The food on the steamtable looked less than appetizing. It could use a touch-up from the makeup department she told herself as her mind drifted to her job. The stunt coordinator had wound up giving her the lion's share of the female stunts, partially because of her close resemblance to Sally, but mainly because of her expertise. When she had finally gotten to see him yesterday, Alex had told her and Pepper that there wasn't enough time to train Pepper to do the more dangerous gags.

Speed. Always speed. She had worked with Alex before, when he was just another stuntman, and had hoped that as their coordinator he was going to be more concerned with safety than with speed. But the way he had talked about his method of awarding the gags had made it clear to Chyna that he was very concerned about remaining on the director's good side. She had been given her assignment with a veiled warning. So much for old friendships.

Chyna remembered that after Neil's accident she had received a lot of kind condolences and offers of help from Neil's friends. But when she had approached them to join her in bringing suit against the studio, as well as the director and Matt, for their gross negligence, suddenly the camaraderie had melted away and she had been left standing alone. Everyone had been afraid, concerned that they might not be able to get any more work. Stuntworkers depended on staying in the good graces of directors and studios for their livelihoods.

She slid onto the end of a wooden bench that had

been set up under a sagging canopy that was meant to fend off the blistering sun. It failed.

Several people smiled and greeted her as she joined them. They all began discussing the picture, and Chyna's thoughts of the past faded away.

The man next to her, the one dressed as a pilot, was beginning to have second thoughts about his dashing image and was shedding parts of his costume. Chyna hid her smile and jabbed at the overfried eggs on her chipped plate. She had time to take only a forkful before Pepper hailed her.

Chyna looked up and saw the blonde walking toward her, flanked by two very able-bodied men. It didn't take Pepper long to find playmates, Chyna thought wryly.

After a quick introduction Pepper casually turned down Chyna's offer to join her for practice and went off with her new friends, Pete and Rick, to explore the island.

Chyna looked after them, shaking her head. She had seen Pepper wavering when she had made her suggestion, but Rick had convinced her that there was no need to practice something she had done so many times before. Chyna had seen his type before: the so-called professional who had a god-complex and thought that he didn't need to go over a stunt. He gave the rest of them a bad name.

Suddenly breakfast was very unappealing. She rose, taking the dull gray tray with her, and went looking for a trash can. She found one and dumped the contents of her tray with a heavy thud.

"It's that bad, eh?"

She turned around to find Matt standing behind her.

"I was just about to get some breakfast. I think you talked me out of it," he said, nodding toward the trash can.

She smiled wryly. "I had no idea I was that persuasive."

Matt looked at her for a long moment, his eyes sparkling. "You strike me as a woman who can be very persuasive when she wants to be."

Now what did he mean by that? Was he referring to the committee she had organized? Or was there another meaning to his words?

"Don't let me dissuade you," she said lightly. "I just seem to have lost my appetite."

"The heat'll do that," Matt commented.

The silence hung clumsily between them, as if each was waiting for the other to say something.

Finally Chyna made an effort, although for the life of her, she didn't know why. "There's always a silver lining to everything. Now I don't have to wait so long before I can go and practice my stunts.

"You're doubling for Sally, aren't you?" he asked, and she nodded. "She goes through some pretty harrowing things in the script," he commented. "That is, you do," he amended.

Chyna grinned. "Thank goodness for that, or else they wouldn't need a stuntwoman and I still wouldn't have a job."

" 'Still'?"

She was surprised at the note of interest in his voice. She would have thought a producer had more important things to do than associate with a stuntworker—especially one who had tried to take him to court.

"I thought you knew everything about me," she

said with a soft laugh. "You made it sound as if you thought you had my number yesterday."

"How long have you been out of work?" he asked.

"Ever since I tried to bring the studio to court," she said evenly.

"That long, eh?"

"That long."

He considered the matter for a moment. "Well, did you learn anything from the experience?"

Learn anything? What did he think she was, a trick dog? "Yes," she said with a toss of her head, slamming the tray down on top of the open trash can. "I learned not to trust the studio brass. Now, if you'll excuse me, I have some heavy practicing to do."

With that she marched off into the surrounding greenery, fervently hoping that she wouldn't get lost.

3

Chyna felt achy.

The humidity had seeped into her joints, making them feel stiff and puffy. Her cheeks felt as if she had a permanent blush embossed on them, and even her eyelashes felt heavy with moisture. The strict concentration she needed to do her stunts was frequently broken by visions of snow-filled scenes dancing before her mind's eye.

It got to the point where she felt she couldn't go on if she didn't have a tall, cold glass of *something*. Calling it a day, Chyna made her way over to the cafeteria. But the people in charge of providing the meals were having their own problems with the weather. The refrigeration system was out, and the coldest thing available was a collection of several large lettuce leaves.

Chyna thought of the beach and her spirits rose

again. With renewed enthusiasm she hurried off to get her bathing suit.

When she got inside her stifling shack she pulled out a gleaming white bikini from her suitcase. Quickly Chyna stripped off her perspiration-soaked clothes and threw them in a small heap on her cot, then slipped on the bikini. It complemented her bronzed tan rather nicely, she thought, looking down at the network of lacing and very little cloth.

She was fully aware of all the looks and appreciative stares she garnered as she walked through the camp to the beach. But then, she reminded herself, there weren't that many things to look at out here in the middle of nowhere.

"Where are you going, darling?"

The voice was familiar. She had heard it piercing the din over and over again all afternoon, uttering cutting, cryptic words. She turned around to look at the puffy, round face of the director and saw the wide, semi-leering smile on his lips fade away into his jowls.

"Oh, it's you," he said, his tone both disappointed and dismissive. "I thought you were Sally." He walked off abruptly, annoyed at his mistake.

"Hello to you, too," Chyna said under her breath. She shook her head and went on.

When she arrived on the beach she found the assistant director and his crew wrapping up a shooting session. On both sides of Chyna miniarmies of extras, all dressed in multicolored native garb that recalled the 1930s, ambled by. Many gave her the once-over and grinned beneath their heavy cocoa-colored makeup.

Water. All she could think of was cool water. Lovely, wet water cascading all over her hot, parched body. Chyna ran into the surf and found that the cold water she had longed for was warm. But at least it wasn't hot, the way everything else was. Reveling in the delicious sensation the water produced, Chyna began to swim further out, willing herself to think of nothing and no one. With her back to the shore she didn't see the one lone figure approaching the beach just as all the others were retreating from it.

The peaceful early morning waters had changed; they were now churning restlessly under the afternoon sun, taking Chyna's breath away and making her exert herself as she tried to maintain control over the direction she was taking. After a few minutes she decided not to swim out too much further. All her practicing had made her tired, and she didn't want to risk being in a position where she might have to struggle against the current to get back.

Just as the thought occurred to her, a large wave washed over her head, sending her underwater and snatching away her breath entirely. Worse than that, it snatched away something else as well.

"Oh, no!" she gasped, bobbing up, one hand running over her naked breasts in horror. Her bikini top! She looked frantically around in all directions, but it wasn't anywhere to be seen. It had disappeared, a casualty of the last wave.

"Anything wrong?"

Matt's voice reached her over the noise of the waves. He was standing at the edge of the water, and she could make out a look of concern on his face—or was he scowling again? Who cared? She had something more important to worry about right now.

"Yes!" she called back.

Then, to her horror, Matt began to wade in toward her. He must have thought she was having trouble swimming, she realized.

"No, stay back!" she cried, swimming a little closer toward shore to keep out of the rougher waters. By now she was thoroughly miserable. What was she going to do? She couldn't just parade back into camp. What an idiot she was for not bringing something with her. A towel, a robe. Anything!

As Chyna bobbed up and down in the water she realized that Matt, who had stopped momentarily to look at her quizzically, was now coming toward her again. Water was steadily lapping up the sides of his jeans, turning them a darker shade of blue. An orphaned thought that this should be filmed by someone came flashing through Chyna's brain. He looked like a masterful warlord stalking a feudal peasant girl who had been promised to him by some penniless, spineless farmer instead of this year's tithe.

"Stop!" she pleaded again as the water came up to his thighs.

"You sound like you're in trouble," he called back to her, but he did as she asked.

Chyna breathed a sigh of relief, then realized that there was nothing to be relieved about. Her predicament hadn't changed.

"I am in trouble," she shouted unhappily.

"Then get out of there!" he ordered.

"I can't!"

"Okay," he said decisively, annoyed with the situation, "then I'm coming in to get you." The waters slapped hungrily at his waist, making him look like an artist's rendition of a young Neptune.

"You can't!"

"Why not?" he demanded impatiently, totally confused by her lack of cooperation.

"Because I'm not dressed!" she retorted in exasperation.

He cocked his head. "Come again?"

The sun danced on his sandy blond head as he waited for an explanation. She could see a smile forming on his lips. He had guessed her problem . . . or could he see her now?

She moved back a little, but the unruly waters made progress difficult. "The water ripped off my top," she finally called out.

"Oh." The single word was loaded with a good many things Chyna didn't want to explore at the moment. "What do you propose we do about it?" he asked, his tone changing to one of amusement.

"Your shirt!" Chyna cried suddenly. "Can I have your shirt?"

He laughed. "First she wants to take me to court, now she wants the shirt off my back." He shook his head. "Some people have a lot of gall." For a moment she was sure he was going to go on tormenting her, but instead she was relieved to see him strip off his shirt. The sun gleamed down on his tanned shoulders, making Chyna's heart quicken of its own accord.

"Wait, go back," she ordered as he began to approach her again.

"Then how are you going to get this shirt?" he wanted to know.

"Turn your back and hold it out. I'll take care of the rest," she told him, watching him carefully.

He did as she asked, and Chyna swam over rapidly,

afraid that he would turn around at the last minute, but he didn't.

After taking the pullover from him, she quickly slipped it over her own shoulders and let it fall about her hips. The water lapped at the ends and inched its way up the fabric. Another wave came, throwing her against Matt.

"Hey, steady now," he cautioned, grabbing her firmly by the shoulders. The momentary touch of their bodies, even with the water between them, had generated a burst of fire through Chyna, and she looked up at him, stunned.

She became conscious of the fact that he was staring at her, and looked down to see just what he was looking at. She might have guessed! His blue pullover was clinging seductively to her breasts.

"We'd . . . um . . . better get you out of here before the waves decide to rip that off you, too . . . not that I'd blame them."

The last part was said in a muttered aside, as if he were talking to himself and not even conscious of having said the words aloud.

Chyna felt embarrassed, and she chided herself for being childish. After all, they were both adults, and this was an accident. It wasn't as if she had planned all this on purpose, or . . . She looked up at his face as he took a firm hold of her elbow and practically marched her out of the water. Just what *was* he thinking?

"I haven't thanked you," she mumbled.

"I'm the one who should thank you," Matt said.

"And just what does that mean?" she asked as they stepped back onto the sand.

"My shirt's never looked so good," he said, a

boyish twinkle coming into his eyes as they once more left her face and skimmed the terrain below her neck.

Chyna crossed her arms over her breasts. "I just might retract my thanks," she said, her voice strained.

"I just might retract my shirt," he countered, reaching for her collar.

"Oh, no, don't do that!" she cried as she felt his fingers brush against her throat. Heat danced across her skin and her nipples tautened.

For a moment there was a potent silence between them. The cry of a faraway sea gull threatened to break the spell, but Matt bent his head toward her, as if moved by some unseen force. Chyna stood rooted to the spot, watching him, yet wondering if any of this was really happening. He slipped his hand along the outline of her jaw and cupped her cheek, touching her throat and neck ever so lightly as he did so. Then he drew her mouth up to his and kissed her, appearing almost as surprised by his action as she was.

Chyna had thought she had sampled all the joys that one could glean from romance. But never in all her experience had she felt anything close to what was bursting upon her senses at that moment. A second before his lips found hers, her heart started pounding wildly. She had the same queasy feeling in her stomach that she felt just before jumping out of a plane without a chute. The exhilarating feeling sped throughout her body with an intensity so great that she dreaded it and yet desired it at the same time. She scarcely knew herself as a tidal wave of desire broke free within her; she was drawn to the surging force of his mouth as if her very life hung in the balance.

Her mind felt clouded, yet she was aware of everything: the feel of his hard chest as it pressed against her heaving breasts; the outline of his urgent body as it moved against hers; and the strangely comforting touch of his hand as it roamed along her back and shoulders, pulling her closer to him until she didn't know where she ended and he began.

Breathing. She wasn't breathing! The thought registered itself suddenly. His kiss had stolen away her breath and played havoc with her senses at the same time. She filled her lungs with air, but the action just added to the heady feeling as she heard the rasping sound of her own ragged breath.

Hardly conscious of what she was doing, Chyna wrapped her arms around Matt's neck, kissing him back as demandingly as she was being kissed. One high wave crashed against them, dragging back some of the sand beneath Chyna's feet and finally breaking the spell that held them in its grip. She blinked several times as Matt let her go. The moment was gone for him as well.

He looked at her solemnly now, his face no longer teasing, his eyes no longer pulling her toward him like powerful magnets. He seemed to be disturbed by what had happened between them.

"I'm sorry," he said.

The words both stung and surprised her. It had been a wonderfully exciting, mystical moment—and he was sorry? Hadn't he felt something happening? Or was it just she? Maybe it was, she thought. Maybe it was just the heat.

Although they didn't look anything alike, there was something in Matt's competent, reserved manner that reminded Chyna painfully of Neil. But there was something more about Matt. Just being near him made her tingle and the tiny hairs on her body stand erect. That had never happened between her and Neil.

But Matt had said he was sorry. Her brain echoed with the word. Why? What had caused him to turn away? It was as if a curtain had fallen over his face. Was it that he thought, just as she did, that any sort of a relationship between them was just asking for trouble? Or was there something else?

"Why are you sorry? Was it so bad?" she heard herself asking. Embarrassed, she turned her flushed face away and looked straight ahead in the direction she was walking.

Quietly, Matt fell into step beside her, shortening his stride in order to keep pace with her. "No, it wasn't," he answered in a low voice. "But I took advantage of the moment."

"Advantage?" she echoed, stunned. She had never expected to hear that from any man, and especially not him. Most men were out to take every advantage they could. Matt sounded as if he came from the Victorian Age. "'Advantage' would have been if you'd dragged me by my hair into a cave and"—she laid the back of her hand across her forehead dramatically—"had your way with me."

Her words succeeded in bringing a small, sensual smile to his lips. The inner thrill returned. At the same time, part of her was wondering what on earth she was doing trying to make Matthew Harrigan feel better. Had she lost her mind?

Matt stopped walking for a moment, standing just on the outskirts of the camp. For a second she thought he was going to kiss her again. But he didn't.

The look in his eyes changed, clouded over by some inner thought. "I've got rushes to see to," he

told her. "Don't go swimming by yourself anymore," he ordered. And then he added with a grin,
"Or at least wear a stronger bathing suit."

Chyna stared after him as he left, feeling tremen-
dously let down. Telling herself that her reaction was
totally illogical didn't help matters any. Neither did the
sudden realization that she was attracting quite a few
stares, standing there in Matt's clinging shirt.

Get back to your shack, dummy, and stop thinking
about him, she told herself, hurrying through the
camp.

She reached her shack in record time.

4

~~~~~~~~~~

Matt's shirt lay on the newly cleaned sink counter where Chyna had tossed it the day before. Each time she passed it, the shirt caught her eye, drawing her attention as if it were a magnet.

"You keep looking at that shirt as if the guy were still in it," Pepper commented as she stretched lazily on her cot, conquered by the late morning sun and a strenuous workout.

Chyna kept rummaging through her clothes, looking for something that hadn't been destroyed by the humidity. "No more high jumps for you," she declared carelessly. "The thin air is scrambling your brain. You're beginning to hallucinate."

Giving up her half-hearted quest, she decided to remain in the shorts and halter top she was wearing, and to return Matt's shirt right away. She slung it over her bare shoulder and headed for the door. "I'd better see about returning this," she said.

Pepper propped herself up on her elbow. "Or filling it," she teased, leaning over.

Chyna tugged at the other woman's arm, pulling it out from under her, and Pepper fell face down on her cot, laughing as if she had uncovered a secret.

"Definitely scrambled," Chyna announced, walking out.

But she grinned as she began walking toward Matt's trailer on the far side of the set. What would he say if she held up his shirt, batted her eyes prettily and murmured, "I'd like a refill, please."

He'd probably say, "Ah, ha, I've won. I've dazzled her. She won't be any more trouble to me," Chyna thought, rolling the scene over in her head. Well, Mr. Harrigan, I don't intend to be any trouble—just as long as you intend to run a safe production. And I also don't intend to be dazzled by you, no matter how cute your cleft chin is. . . .

Chyna stopped abruptly. He had a cleft chin? When had she noticed that? *Why* had she noticed that? Maybe a little dazzle was slipping in, despite her efforts not to let it. The shirt began to feel heavier on her shoulder. The sooner she rid herself of anything belonging to Matt Harrigan, the better, she decided.

Ribbons of color were fanning out across the sky, stretching until they merged with the light haze of blue and disappeared. The idyllic scene above was in direct contrast to what was transpiring below. The air was blue there, too, but for another reason. As Chyna approached the area where the film crew had been working for several hours, setting up for a shot that would last less than six seconds on the screen, she heard the director's voice thundering above the din.

"Damn it, are we going to fall behind schedule

already?" he demanded of the world at large. The world wasn't answering him. But his glare finally prodded an unwilling reply from Alex.

"He just needs a little more time to practice," the stunt coordinator explained, nodding toward the man under discussion.

"What's to practice?" Dussault demanded, waving his arms around. In his furor he also managed to save himself from a low-flying mosquito that had been about to use his bald head as a landing strip, Chyna noticed, coming closer. "He's either got it down or he doesn't," Dussault groused. "The pads'll absorb most of the wear anyway. Now, does he do it, or do we get someone else?" He crossed his arms in front of him, glaring over the bridge of his hawklike nose.

Chyna saw the muscles around the stuntman's mouth twitch slightly. She knew what was at stake here. The man didn't want to be labeled a trouble-maker. Directors, she thought wryly, don't hire trou-blemakers. They avoid them. And being avoided makes it tough to eat. Especially if you only know one trade. There isn't much call for people who only know how to crash cars.

Chyna leaned against a tree, watching, knowing that she had other things to do, knowing that she had promised herself not to pay attention to anyone's work but her own. But she couldn't help herself.

"I'll be ready in a minute," the stuntman said quietly.

A triumphant look came over the director's face. "That's more like it," he said, a satisfied smile spreading over his wide mouth. He turned to see Chyna watching him. "What the hell are you doing here?" he demanded.

"Watching," she answered lightly.

"You're not in this scene," Dussault snapped dismissively.

"I know that," she said, not moving. "I thought I might pick up some pointers."

Her answer and her tone irritated Dussault. "I thought you said she was the best," he growled at Alex.

Alex opened his mouth to offer an excuse when Chyna cut in for him. "That's how you stay the best," she said, keeping her voice light. "By watching and concentrating. It's what keeps you alive."

The expression on her face was the embodiment of sweetness, but it didn't fool Dussault. It wasn't meant to. He spun on his heel and stormed off, not saying a word, leaving a gaping crowd behind him. Chyna moved away from the tree she had been leaning against. "I guess you've got time to practice now," she said to the stuntman before she walked away.

"Chyna," Alex called after her.

She stopped, but didn't turn around. She knew what was coming. Absently she hooked her finger into the collar of Matt's shirt and played with it, waiting for Alex to catch up to her.

"I told you that I didn't want any trouble out of you," he warned.

Chyna bit her tongue. She wasn't used to being spoken to this way. What she wanted to say was that it was Alex's obligation to stand up for his people, not let them be browbeaten into doing gags they weren't ready for. But she kept her words to herself, chewing on the inside of her mouth.

"No trouble," she said finally. "I'm the soul of cooperation." She offered him a big smile. And then the smile turned serious. "Why didn't you say something to Dussault instead of siding with him?" she asked bluntly. Someday, Chyna, you're going to get the gift of eloquence—or else someone is going to wind up feeding you your teeth, she thought. But she didn't retract her question.

"Chyna, stay out of what you don't know. It was up to Rick to be ready. Dussault is only working according to the schedule."

He left, muttering something inaudible under his breath, and Chyna let out a big sigh. Maybe Alex was right. She had noticed that Rick had a penchant for not practicing. Hadn't he lured Pepper away that first day? When was she going to learn to keep quiet? Well, no damage had been done, she told herself. And maybe Rick had learned his lesson about the need to practice.

Forget it, Chyna. They don't need a den mother and nobody likes a person who butts in all the time. She decided to put the incident out of her mind. She had a shirt to return.

"That broad's got to go," Dussault railed at Matt, bringing his fist down on Matt's desk and causing a minor earthquake that caused several piles of paper to collapse.

He couldn't bring himself to regard her as "that broad," but Matt had known immediately who Dussault was referring to when the director had stormed into the trailer and made his demand. An image of Chyna, his wet shirt clinging to her supple body, came back to him. "Take it easy, Phil," he said soothingly.

"Phillip," the director corrected haughtily. "I can't work with her looking over my shoulder, making notes every time I tell some sniveling stuntman to earn his oversized paycheck."

"She was taking notes?" Matt asked, his voice more serious. Was she out to start trouble already?

"Well, not exactly, but I could see by the way she was looking that she's making notes," Dussault said evasively, although his outrage didn't abate any.

"Oh," Matt said, relief lacing his tone. "Mental notes."

"Yeah, 'mental notes.' Mental notes, shmental notes, what's the difference? She's trouble. Look at all the problems she caused you last year."

But Matt put his hand up, stopping the other man from going on. Why he felt compelled to defend her was a mystery to him, but he didn't like Dussault's tone. "That was over her husband—" he began.

"So, she could've worn black like any other widow and kept her mouth shut. I warn you, Matt, she's gonna be nothing but trouble for us." The director's voice echoed in the enclosed area like an omen of doom.

"She comes highly recommended and we need her," Matt reminded the shorter man, trying to hold on to his patience.

Dussault took umbrage with Matt's laid-back attitude. He pulled back his shapeless shoulders, sticking out a barrel chest that had long since sunk down to his pants line. "Just keep her away from me," he ordered.

"Don't worry," Matt promised, rising. He put his hand reassuringly on Dussault's shoulder. "I'll take care of her."

Oh, no, you won't, Chyna thought as his words floated out to her through the trailer door she had just opened. She had arrived on the scene just in time to overhear the last bit of conversation. It confirmed her gnawing suspicions of Matt's genial attitude toward her. He was hoping, no doubt, to keep her quiet by taking advantage of the tropical setting and romancing her. After all, a woman with love on her mind wouldn't have time for anything else, right? she thought with a cryptic smlie. Well, Mr. Producer, sir, you are in for one hell of an awakening, she promised him as she sidestepped Dussault. I'm not about to fall in love with you.

The director looked surprised to see her. He also looks as if he wishes he were driving a tank, Chyna thought, amused. She nodded toward him, then turned to walk into the trailer.

For a moment the air conditioning was a shock to her whole system. It felt as if she had just stepped through the looking glass into another world. It took her a moment to get acclimated to it. And then it took her another moment to get acclimated to Matt. Why did he have to be so breathtakingly good-looking? she thought. But then, if he wasn't, he probably wouldn't think he had much of a chance of distracting her from any transgressions that might be going on during the filming.

Just a man, Chyna. Ninety-eight percent of that is all water. Water never looked so good, she decided.

He looked surprised to see her. He also looked pleased. Come into my parlor, said the spider to the fly, Chyna thought. Except this time the fly had come willingly—bearing a shirt. She suddenly recalled the object of her mission and reached for it.

"I've brought back your shirt," she said, holding it out to him.

He took it, using the opportunity to take hold of her hand as well. "Thank you," he said softly. The words, though simple, still managed to curl their way into the pit of her stomach, making it queasy. "Why don't you sit down?" he suggested, nodding toward the beige sofa under the window.

"No, I—" She began to make a million excuses. Being in a small area with Matt wasn't wise. She wasn't a fool. She knew when she was in trouble. But the idea of staying was so appealing. . . .

"You look like you're ready to take flight," he commented.

Chyna lifted her chin. That had decided her, and she settled down on the sofa. He wasn't slow in joining her, and he chose the same side as she did.

"Don't you think you need a little more room?" she asked, meeting the challenge in his eyes.

"This is fine," he told her, smiling. It was a perfect smile. The kind, she thought, that was bought from some beaming orthodontist. Still, in this case the end justified the means. His smile *was* beautiful, no matter what its origin. Think about something else, she ordered herself. She looked down at his shoes. Scuffed. He was human.

"Have you eaten?" he asked, suddenly breaking her concentration.

She shook her head, her scalp tingling as her hair began to dry in the cool atmosphere. At least she assumed the tingling sensation was from the air conditioning. "The line's too long," she explained, looking for a safe topic. "I figured I'd fry before it was my turn to order a dead tuna on rye."

"Then share this with me," he suggested, taking her hand and rising.

Just what was it that he wanted her to share? she wondered warily, ready for anything. But all he did was lead her to a small table with two chairs. Beams of sunlight streamed through the window, dancing along the long silver tray that stood in the center of the table, still covered.

"You believe in living well, don't you?" she couldn't help commenting.

"Whenever I can," he answered. "I've earned it." His tone was utterly straightforward.

"I'm really not up to eating," she protested, trying to pull her hand free. For some strange reason the touch of his hand made her feel very vulnerable. "This heat has killed my appetite. It's a wonder all the people on the island aren't forty-pound weaklings."

He didn't seem to be listening to her as he used his free hand to uncover the tray. A tempting array of crabmeat, shrimp and scallops reminded her that there was some life left to her appetite after all.

"This, I take it, didn't come from the lunch trucks," Chyna said.

Matt laughed. It was a delicious, compelling laugh that made her feel good. "No, I had it brought in from the city," he confessed.

Chyna deposited herself in one of the chairs. "I don't blame you," she said. "The food on the trucks is pretty awful. But it's either that or starve," she said philosophically. "And it's kind of a long way to brown-bag it." He was still holding her hand. She raised her brows as she looked at him. "Do I ever get to use this again?" she asked, glancing down at her captive hand. His skin felt warm against hers, despite the air conditioning. Despite a lot of things. "I need it for my knife," she added.

"Which I trust will be applied only to your lunch," he said, finally releasing her hand.

"Meaning?" she asked, beginning to eat. She wasn't going to make this easy for him if he was planning on a lecture. As far as she was concerned, she had done less than nothing. And definitely not enough to merit Dussault's fury.

"Meaning that Dussault says you're driving him crazy."

She speared a shrimp and dipped it in cocktail sauce before she answered. "It's not a drive," she said casually, taking a bite. "It's a short putt."

She noticed that Matt had to struggle to keep back a grin. "Dussault's an excellent director," Matt told her. "His methods may be a little hard to put up with at times, but he gets results—and," he added, leaning forward, "his bark is a lot worse than his bite. I've worked with him before. He knows what he's doing."

She nodded her head absently. There was no point in debating the subject. And maybe Matt was right. Maybe she was just being overly sensitive. Time would tell.

"But of course, I'm not a fanatic on the subject. If you have any complaints about the way Dussault is handling the stunts, come to me, okay? I don't relish having him unduly upset, or seeing my set become the scene of screaming matches. Fair enough?"

"*I* don't scream," she said quietly, but she smiled. "Fair enough," she echoed. At least, it *sounded* fair enough, she added silently.

He sat down and regarded her thoughtfully for a moment. She looked over at his empty plate. "Has the food been tampered with?" she asked lightly. "Is that how you get rid of potential problems?" she posed. "You feed them a last meal that's been laced with cyanide?" She pretended to sniff the rest of the food on her plate. "Funny, I don't smell any almonds." She looked up at him, her eyes twinkling. "That's what cyanide's supposed to smell like, isn't it? Almonds? Or did you use something else?"

"Nothing else," he assured her. "The food's fine. See?" To prove his point he took a golden scallop and consumed it in one bite. "I wouldn't use anything as crude as poison on you. You're too valuable."

So you're going to sweep me off my feet and off my guard, she thought with a smile. Well, put your broom away, Matt Harrigan. I don't fool that easily. She retired her fork. Time for the game to end before he decided that she was going to be dessert. She needed this job and didn't want to be put in the position of having to say no to any propositions. She glanced toward the door.

"In a hurry?" he asked.

She nodded. "As a matter of fact, yes. I promised Pepper I'd—"

"Pepper," he echoed. "Chyna. Don't you people have real names?" he marveled.

"Chyna *is* my real name," she said, taking exception to his supercilious tone. "My father was a history professor at Cal State, Fullerton. He loved the Orient."

"He must have been thrilled when you told him you'd decided to risk your neck for a living," he commented. He thought of his own daughter and how he would react if she told him she wanted to be a stuntwoman. Of course, at five, that was some distance in the future . . .

He realized that Chyna was withdrawing from him

slightly. The expression on her face told him that she thought he was laughing at her. "As a matter of fact, he raised me to be a free thinker," she said with just a hint of resentment. "To try my hand at anything that moved me."

Something drove him on to comment, "So you decided to try legalized suicide."

Chyna pushed her plate away. "Where would you be without us legalized suicidees?" she asked, wondering why he was baiting her this way. He's trying to confuse you, she warned herself. He was succeeding admirably.

"Probably making movies that were relegated to second-rate theaters for limited runs that no one would attend," he admitted. He wasn't sure just what had made him say what he had about stunt work. But he had found himself going over the script earlier that morning, picking out the dangerous stunts Chyna was slated to perform. She would be facing death no fewer than eight times. For the first time the idea bothered him. He wondered if having Chyna around had brought back the specter of last year's accident. "Don't get me wrong, you perform a very necessary service," he told her. "I just always thought of stuntmen as, well, men."

"The proper term," she informed him, amused, "is stuntworker or stuntperson. Use the word 'stuntman' again and I'll report you to the nearest women's lib chapter," she threatened, hardly bothering to check the smile blossoming on her lips.

"I'd rather you looked into the matter personally," he said, leaning toward her over the table.

Too close for comfort. Time to retreat, she told herself, pushing back her chair. To her dismay, he rose with her. "Thanks for lunch," she said cheerfully, although the words sounded strained.

"You hardly touched it."

"I ate more than you did," she pointed out.

He stopped her at the door, one arm barricading her into the trailer. "I had other things on my mind."

No doubt, she thought. As she looked up into his eyes, she saw exactly what those other things were. Her pulse went up a notch, just the way it did before she hurled herself off a cliff. Same difference, she thought, except in this case there was no springboard waiting to break her fall, no air mattress to cradle her. A woman could break her neck like this—or something else.

Searching for a way to avoid the inevitable, she looked down at the desk. Her eyes fell on a framed photograph.

"Who's that?" she asked suddenly.

Matt pulled his head back. Saved! Chyna thought in relief. "That's my daughter," he said. There was no mistaking the fondness in his voice.

"Is she home, with your wife?" Chyna asked, emphasizing the last word. She knew next to nothing about this man and naturally assumed that he came equipped with a family neatly tucked away somewhere out of sight.

"No," Matt answered. "With the housekeeper. I don't know who's home with my wife. My ex-wife," he corrected. "Actually, she's probably not home at all. That was part of the problem," he said, sounding so coldly indifferent that Chyna wondered if he had ever cared for the woman.

"Refused to stay home like a good little wife, did

she?" Chyna asked, thinking back to his comment about stuntmen. He was probably a card-carrying chauvinist of the first degree. With looks like that, why not? she thought. Women probably threw themselves all over him, hoping that he could further their careers and make their dreams come true. Why should he have any respect for women at all?

She stopped herself, wondering whose side she was arguing, his or hers.

"No, as a matter of fact, Laura wanted a career more than she wanted me or Meredith" he said flatly, his face showing no expression whatsoever.

So that was it, she thought. That was what was responsible for the bitterness that she saw in him from time to time. She wondered how much he had loved his wife and how hurt he had been when she turned her back on him. "I'm sorry," she said quietly. "Sometimes I'm a little too flip for my own good. I . . ." I'm tripping over my tongue again, she thought desperately.

Mercifully, he accepted her apology quickly enough. His eyes swept over her warmly. "I'm not used to women who'll admit it when they're wrong," he said, touching her hair. His fingers buried themselves in the silkiness he found there, gently touching her scalp. The tingling sensation was back, she noted with alarm.

"I'm not afraid of admitting that I'm wrong," Chyna said, trying to meet him on equal footing. "When I am."

"No?" he asked, studying her face. The blueness of her eyes captivated him.

"No," she said. It sounded like a pulsating whisper.

"What *are* you afraid of, Chyna O'Brien?" he asked, his voice like velvet. He cupped the back of her head in his hand, tilting it just a little.

You, she wanted to say, the thought springing to her mind. You represent something that frightens me, something that has nothing to do with faulty equipment or gags that go sour.

"Not much," she lied, wondering if he noticed that the pulse in her throat was throbbing wildly.

He lowered his mouth until it was just a breath away from hers, teasing her. "I'm glad," he said, his words gliding along the outline of her lips.

She wanted to say that she was in a hurry. She wanted to say that Pepper was waiting for her. She wanted to say that she had to go practice her gags. She wanted to say a lot of things that didn't get said just then.

It's hard to say anything when your mouth is otherwise occupied.

5

As his mouth moved over hers, evoking a thousand pleasures, Chyna felt as if a Pandora's box of emotions had opened within her. Vainly she tried to shut the lid. She didn't want to feel anything. Not for him. All he was trying to do was distract her. There was nothing else behind this kiss but business.

Why did business have to feel this good?

She had to stop this, she told herself. But all she did was sink deeper into the pleasure of Matt's kiss. A moment longer, just a moment longer, something within her pleaded, something that was enjoying this immensely.

You're kissing him back, her brain telegraphed to her. You're giving him the wrong idea. You're making him think you like it.

It was hard not to like having every fiber of your body tingle with electrifying excitement, she thought as her sanity faded away.

Slowly Matt massaged the contours of her slim back, delicately exploring the slope of her shoulder blades and rimming the lower edge of her halter top. Involuntarily Chyna shivered.

The air conditioning. The air conditioning was making her shiver. She would make sure he understood that—if only she could regain control of her lips. But they were still being laid siege to. And still hungrily giving back as good as they got. It was as if she had no say in the matter.

Chyna's arms wound around Matt's neck, making her body stretch against him. As he pressed her to him, Chyna felt the outline of his hard muscles. This was no soft executive given to relishing the comforts of life. He honed his body in the same manner he honed his production—with an eye out for every minute detail.

But details were beginning to fade into oblivion, forced urgently away by the wild, churning sensations he awoke in her. It had been a long time since anyone had loved her.

No!

The last thought brought her back to her senses before she allowed the roller coaster to take her to the crest of her desire. And before it went down the long valley, flying out of control.

She struggled to regain her breath. Slowly, breathe in slowly, she instructed herself. Don't look like a panting puppy in front of him. He told that troll of a director that he would take care of you. Don't let him think he did it with one silly kiss.

But it hadn't been a silly kiss, her racing pulse insisted. It had been a poem. A poem? It had been an entire epic. And she had loved it. There was definite danger here, she thought. The man's mouth was lethal.

She tried to summon a blasé look. It didn't quite match her flushed cheeks. "Taking advantage again?" she asked, hoping that she sounded amused instead of breathless.

"No," Matt said, smiling into her eyes. It was as if he saw right through her, damn him. "Not this time."

He was stroking her. His hands were at his sides, yet he was stroking her, she thought incredulously. His eyes were like liquid magic. She had to get out of there before she did something that one of them was going to regret a lot. Namely her.

"Sure you won't stay?" he coaxed, this time reaching up and sliding a finger along the ridge of her jaw.

Was this how Napoleon felt when he arrived at Waterloo? she wondered. Well, at least she was going to be able to retreat. And she fully intended to. She groped behind her, searching for the doorknob. Eureka.

"I'm sure," she said, her voice sounding incredibly calm, despite the turmoil that was going on inside her, "I have to get—"

He reached around behind her, placing his hand over hers, snatching freedom away once again. His warmth penetrated not only her hand, but her senses, telling her that no matter how she fought it, she liked being touched by this man.

Primitive approach, primitive reactions, she tried to tell herself. But something in her wasn't buying it. She knew herself too well.

"Chyna."

It was the first time he had called her by name, and it gave her a thrill. For an unguarded moment she wondered what it would sound like, coming from his lips, uttered with the thickness of deep desire. *Get hold of yourself, Chyna! You're letting the romance of the movie affect you. Serves you right for staying up last night and reading the entire script.*

"What?" she asked. She tried to make the word sound like a challenge. *I'm not going to make this easy for you,* she thought with ebbing determination. *I'm not. No one's seducing me just to keep me quiet.*

His voice was low, melodic. Thrilling. "Why don't we just go along being exceptionally wary and cautious with one another . . . and see what develops?" he suggested.

It was a line that would have fit right into the movie, she thought. And it was just a line. So why did she feel like a pat of butter on a hot skillet?

Calling on all her powers of concentration, Chyna managed to block out some of her feelings. "Nothing is going to develop," she said with firm control, "except, I hope, a good movie that's utterly trouble free." *Good. Strike a blow for your side,* she told herself, feeling just the tiniest bit smug.

She watched him, expecting to see constrained annoyance in his eyes because she wasn't taking his cue and falling into his arms. Instead he looked amused. She didn't know whether to take exception to that or not. *The man plays a hell of a confusing game,* she thought with a touch of admiration. She just wished it wasn't at her expense.

"That, too," he said, laughing softly. "But I wasn't quite thinking of the movie just at this moment."

She wished he'd let her out of this tiny space. He was so close that he was making it difficult for her to compete in this verbal tennis match. "Oh, weren't you?" she asked a bit sarcastically. "I thought I heard that the movie is always uppermost in your mind." She hoped she sounded flippant enough. Anything but eager.

"I'd be lying if I said it wasn't important," he told her, and she gave him an A for sounding sincere. He must have picked up a few acting tips along the way, she reasoned. "But I'd be a robot if that was all that occupied my mind a hundred percent of the time." He took her hand and placed it on his chest. "Do I feel like a robot to you?"

The look in his eyes was teasing, yet she could have sworn that there was something somber there, too. Was she just imagining it? Or wishing for it? Wishing? Oh, no, that had a lot more connotations to it than she cared to delve into at the moment—at any moment.

She tried to pull back her hand, not wanting any further physical contact with him. But he held it fast against his chest. She felt the excitement flowing through her. Just as she was sure he wanted her to. This whole thing was going to take an awful lot of willpower on her part.

"I don't know" she said lightly. "I'm not sure what a robot is supposed to feel like. I've heard that they've come up with some pretty realistic-looking ones—with all the right working parts," she added humorously.

"I assure you, I'm not a robot." His voice surrounded her like silk.

She pushed him back, although not as hard as she would have liked to. After all, he *was* the producer, and she did want to maintain a working relationship with him, she told herself. "I'll take your word for it," she said, this time managing to swing the door open behind her and escape.

There wasn't any other word for it. She escaped, escaped before his seductive manner broke through her hastily constructed barriers. He certainly wasn't acting the way she had initially expected him to. When she had found out that he was going to be the producer of *The Adventurer,* she had prepared herself for a gruff, blustering man who barked out orders and assumed the attitude that he was ruling by divine right. She could have handled that. This was a good deal more unnerving. But his goal was the same, she told herself. He wanted to render her docile, incapable of doing any harm to his picture no matter what went on during the filming. Well, no matter what his ploy, the man was in for a big surprise, she promised herself as she wove her way through a gaggle of extras who were still lined up waiting to play Russian Roulette with the food that was being offered.

What she couldn't seem to weave her way through was the wall of intolerable heat. It was all around her, sticky and oppressive, making it hard for her to breathe. There was a lot of that going around lately, she thought wryly.

Everyone around her looked as if they were wilting. It was hard to work up any enthusiasm for doing something strenuous when you were surrounded by lethargic-looking people who appeared to have glue in their veins. Chyna searched the area for Pepper. She finally found the other woman sitting cross-legged on the ground, away from everybody else.

"Where've you been?" Pepper asked as Chyna sank down next to her. "I waited as long as I could."

"I got held up," Chyna said evasively. She looked at her friend's fast-disappearing hamburger. "I take it you're in no mood to practice now."

Pepper shook her head, polishing off the last bit, then denuding her fingers of any extra ketchup. "Not now. If I move, I'm going to throw up," she moaned.

"Lovely imagery," Chyna commented dryly. She got up, brushing away several insects that had decided to get to know her better. "Well, we can at least plot out your gag. A little mental rehearsal won't hurt you."

Pepper looked a little uncertain about moving anything at that moment. "I dunno, Chyna," she muttered.

But Chyna wanted someone around to help get her mind off other things, things that flourished in air-conditioned trailers. "C'mon, it'll do you good," she urged, extending her hand to the other woman.

Reluctantly Pepper took her hand and got up.

For the next few days Chyna tried to do nothing but concentrate on her upcoming stunts. She spent hours getting herself in condition, and made it a point to examine all her equipment daily for signs of wear. She could only approximate some of the conditions that would be involved in the actual stunts. Some things would not come into play until the cameras were actually rolling. The exploding gasoline tanks, for instance. There was no way to physically practice for them. It was to be a one-shot take. If she missed, there'd be no second chance. Not unless she suddenly sprouted wings.

Pepper sat watching Chyna work out on the trampoline. Tired, she had opted for a break, but Chyna had doggedly gone on. Behind them loomed the mountain that Chyna was to use in her leap. As far as mountains went, it wasn't all that tall. It would never make the inside of *National Geographic,* Chyna had thought when she had first seen it. But an unprepared fall from any height could kill you.

So could not concentrating, she told herself, feeling her mind trying to drift to other subjects. To one other subject, she amended. Matt Harrigan. As in trouble. She was irritated with herself. Usually she had the ability to shut out absolutely everything that was going on and simply apply herself to the gag at hand. But ever since he had kissed her in his trailer, Matt's rugged face had kept appearing in her mind at totally inopportune, unbidden moments. Like now.

She missed her footing and wound up landing on her rump.

Pepper leaped to her feet and ran over. "What's the matter?" she asked, looking concerned.

Chyna watched the way Pepper nibbled on her lower lip. The other woman was worried about this gag, she could tell. Well, it was a growing club, Chyna thought, not exactly feeling blasé about it herself. "It was just a misstep," she said, waving away Pepper's distress.

"You?" Pepper asked, wide-eyed.

"Me," Chyna laughed, trying to keep the situation light. "I'm not perfect, you know."

She saw the way Pepper eyed the mountain. "Maybe you'd better not try that gag," she suggested hesitantly.

Chyna swung off the trampoline and put a comforting arm around Pepper. "I'm not going to 'try' it," she corrected her. "I'm going to do it. 'Trying' will only get me fried."

In her mind's eye she saw the whole gag in vivid, breathtaking color. Sally was to look appropriately brave for the camera, then step back as Chyna took her place, clutching a rifle in her hands. Taking a running leap, she was to clear a group of exploding gasoline tanks and land on a hidden spring ramp that would catapult her to safety. All very nice, very smooth—*if* it worked.

It would work, she assured herself. There was only one way to face the kind of work she did: with confidence based on the knowledge that she had done everything in her power to pull it off and insure her own safety. The rest was up to luck. And her luck had held for six years.

Pepper, usually so nonchalant about their work, looked unconvinced. "Maybe if you tell Dussault that it's too dangerous . . ." she began, her voice trailing off. "I've got a bad feeling about this, Chyna."

Superstition, Chyna knew, played a large part in the stunt world. "That's all he'd need to hear. He'd be more than thrilled to dump me for loss of nerve," Chyna said with a dry laugh, trying to kid Pepper out of her mood. She got back up on the trampoline. "Don't look so worried. If it wasn't so dangerous, I wouldn't be getting twenty thousand dollars for doing it. And the public wouldn't be clutching at their armrests for a second." That was about how long the shot was going to last on screen: one heartbeat. For that, her own heart was going to stay in her throat until the gag was completed.

Chyna swung back up on the trampoline and began the last part of her workout with renewed vigor, blotting out everything else.

Chyna's first gag was to be one of the action highlights of the movie, and it was one of the main reasons she had gotten hired. She thought about that as she lay on her cot, staring unseeingly into the darkness. It must be about three in the morning, she thought, listening to the sounds of the tropical night. Nothing moved except the mosquitoes in search of cooperative, dormant meals. She knew that it would be hours until the pearl colors of dawn would touch the sky. The crew would be up and around before then, setting up for her shot.

Chyna sat up, knowing that she was too keyed up to drop off to sleep again. An excited knot was taking over all the available space in her stomach.

"It's just another gag," she whispered to herself. Yes, just like Matt Harrigan is just another man.

The wayward thought made her eyes fly open. None of that, she chastised herself sternly. Not today. She decided to busy herself with the mechanics of getting ready.

After wrestling with the pump Chyna succeeded in generating a thin trickle of water. Cupping her hands, she waited patiently to capture enough to wash her face, or at least get the top layer of perspiration off.

That's what it's all about, she thought. Patience. And timing. "Lord, let the timing be right," she murmured. She had done all she could to perfect the routine. The rest was entirely up to her skill and the right conditions. And a little extra help. She closed her eyes and murmured a fleeting prayer she had learned a long time ago. Angels watched over fools and children, right? Which was she?

She had succeeded in bringing a smile to her own lips. A shower would make her feel even better, she decided, making her way through the dusky shack. She found a towel and slung it over her shoulder. At least she wasn't going to have to wait in line today, she thought blissfully, picking up a pair of shorts and a blouse that were lying nearby.

Because of the hour, she didn't bother changing out of her short nightgown. Instead she made her way quickly to the makeshift stalls. She was engrossed in going over the logistics of her stunt, which was why she didn't hear the water running or wonder why there was light showing beneath the large brown tent. She was too caught up in her own thoughts. Pushing the door open, she marched briskly in and stopped dead in her tracks, a gasp hovering in her throat.

Matt's startled smile greeted her. More than that, Matt's wet body greeted her. At least, the parts of it that weren't hidden by the partition did. There were three stalls in the tent, but Chyna didn't see past the first one.

He stopped what he was doing and came up close to the partition. "C'mon in," he invited sensuously. "The water's fine."

Behind him the steady stream of water from the showerhead continued, as if to reinforce his words.

"This isn't Japan," she heard herself saying. "Communal bathing isn't in."

"We could start a new tradition," he told her with the sexiest wink she had ever encountered in her life.

The knot in her stomach tightened. She began to retreat, then stopped herself. She couldn't keep running like this. It wasn't in her nature, and he'd think that he had succeeded in unnerving her. "What are you doing here?" she demanded.

"Taking a shower," he answered cheerfully, beginning to soap himself. As he bent down slightly, Chyna could imagine the path his hands were following. She felt herself getting warmer. As if she needed to be warmer!

"But it's three in the morning," she pointed out.

"You're up," she heard him answer from within the stall.

"I have a gag today," she said, resisting the urge to come closer and look in—just to be able to address his face, of course, she added.

Matt's head popped back up. He was frowning slightly. "I know."

Was he worried that something would go wrong? she wondered. Probably afraid she'd bring another suit against him if it did. "Don't you have a shower in that white-walled palace of yours?" she asked.

Her reference to his trailer brought back his smile. "Yes, I do," he acknowledged, continuing to lather himself. "But it's not working right. I'm going to have to get someone out to look at it," he told her. "I live in mortal fear of having the air conditioning go out on me," he confided with a wink.

"Wouldn't want to see you enduring the elements like the rest of us," she murmured with a touch of sarcasm.

"You're welcomed to share my trailer anytime you

70

want," he said. His grin spread. "Anytime." He turned his back to her for a moment. "Do my back?" he asked.

Chyna stared at the bar of soap he held aloft for her. Not on your life, fella, she thought, making absolutely no move toward him. "Sorry," she quipped. "I don't do windows, or producers."

He shrugged good-naturedly as he turned back around. "My sweat-stained back is on your conscience," he said.

She nodded her head solemnly. "I'll try to live with it," she promised.

Matt returned the soap to its perch and angled his body beneath the showerhead, letting the fine mist dowse him. Chyna watched the water swirl around his feet, taking the white lather with it. She realized that he was watching her watching him, and a blush stung her cheeks as she raised her eyes back to his face.

Matt pulled his towel off the side partition and began drying himself off. "Sure I can't interest you in sharing these facilities with me?" he asked. "They say sharing helps you learn a lot about the other person."

"And what is it you'd want to learn about me?" she asked, knowing that her words sounded coy. Let him think she was playing along—at least for the moment.

"Well," he said brightly, rubbing the towel over his damp dark-blond hair, "I've already learned that you favor short nightgowns," he said, eyeing her. "And so do I—at least on you."

She had forgotten all about the fact that she was standing there in her pajamas. She tilted her head up, like a warrior in battle, refusing to retreat. "Would you mind hurrying up? I'd like to take my shower—alone," she emphasized.

"Your wish is my command," he said, beginning to swing the door open.

Quickly she turned her back. "I'll let you put your clothes on in private," she told him, not knowing exactly what he had in mind. This teasing, bantering Matt Harrigan was totally different from the man who had kissed her on the beach, the man who had apologized for taking advantage. The only thing that remained the same was the undercurrent of sensuality. He was an utter puzzle to her.

"Very decent of you."

Was that a touch of mockery in his voice? "One of us has to be," she retorted. Open mouth, insert foot, she thought. Oh, well, maybe her answer would put him off enough to make it clear that she wasn't interested in any games, and that she wasn't going to be bowled over by a naked, dripping man, even if he was gorgeous. Which he was. Very. Enough, Chyna, enough. You're reacting just the way he wants you to. Just the way he promised Dussault you would.

That did the trick immediately. Suddenly she was sane again.

She found herself growing impatient. He was taking too long. The silence mocked her, daring her to turn around. But she stayed where she was, studying the dull brown tent flap and trying not to let the fact that she was in close proximity to a compellingly handsome, naked man undo her.

Finally Chyna cleared her throat. "Are you finished yet?"

"That's a matter of opinion," Matt said. His voice sounded almost too seductive for words. "I could say that I haven't even begun yet."

"Mr. Harrigan," Chyna said, "I—"

"Considering the circumstances, I think you could call me Matt."

"The circumstances would be a whole lot better if you got your clothes on," she said, hoping that she sounded sufficiently irritated. It was getting hard carrying on this conversation with a tent flap.

"That too is a matter of opinion," he said.

He was directly behind her. The scent of soap, mixed with his own very masculine essence, came wafting through the heavy air, filling her senses. The next thing she knew, his hands were on her shoulders.

6

He turned her around slowly. "Your shower awaits, milady," he said grandly. There was a twinkle in his eyes.

For an instant she let her eyes roam over his well-developed chest. A few drops of water still clung to the fine layer of hair, glistening in the dim artificial light. Producers weren't supposed to look so enticing. Chyna took a deep breath. "Thank you," she said tersely. "Now, if you'll excuse me," she went on, using the most impersonal voice she could muster, considering the situation, "I'd like to take my shower before this area becomes the center of a crowd scene."

She saw that he was letting his gaze wander over her barely hidden curves. With a touch of satisfied pride she could tell that he liked what he saw. Pride? she thought, suddenly coming to. Chyna, get hold of yourself. It's three in the morning and you're standing in your pajamas in front of a very unsettling man.

"You're not moving," she pointed out. Wasn't he ever going to go? "You can't stay here while I take my shower," she insisted.

"I'm the producer," he told her. "I can stay anywhere I want."

He was having fun at her expense. Well, two could play that game, she thought. "Fine," she declared, turning away and heading toward the tent flap. "If anyone wants you, I'll tell them you're guarding the shower—which you wouldn't have to do if you had told the grips to build a separate one for the women."

Strong fingers clamped around her wrist, preventing her departure. Chyna turned to face him and saw that his expression was still mild, amused. "Then we would have missed this little encounter. Tell me, do you always get angry so quickly?"

"Only when I'm hot and gritty—and someone decides to withhold my water," she said, lifting her chin. He had made her lose her temper, and that made her even more annoyed. Usually she was extremely even tempered, but this weather was enough to drive anybody crazy. And now she had this half-nude producer bent on her seduction—or whatever.

Matt walked back over to the first stall and flipped on the faucet. "Your water," he said with a sweep of his hand. And then he walked out of the tent, shaking his head. "My father told me that if I became a producer, I could have anything I wanted. . . ."

Chyna stared at the tent flap even after it had fallen back into place. She thought she had detected a self-mocking tone in his words, but she wasn't sure. All she was sure of was the word "want." She told herself again that it was all an act, all a silly little plan to make her fall for him and keep her mind off watching Dussault. But there was an excitement building within her that wasn't listening to any words. None of hers, at any rate. It was feeding on the uncontrolled tingling sensations that kept springing up each time she was near Matt.

"You're probably allergic to him," she muttered vehemently. In her extreme frustration, she said the words aloud.

"I certainly hope not."

Chyna dropped her bar of soap as his voice came floating through from the other side of the makeshift tent.

She took the rest of her quick shower in utter silence.

Rubbing furiously, she tried to dry herself off. All she succeeded in doing was getting rid of the heaviest layer of water. The tropical humidity insisted on leaving a fine blanket of moisture on her skin. Chyna struggled into the clothes she had brought with her. The shorts refused to slide up her damp legs, sticking to her skin every inch of the way.

"Damn this weather," she muttered impatiently, then realized that the weather wasn't completely responsible for the way she was feeling. Hurriedly she buttoned her blouse, only to look down and realize that she had misaligned the buttons with the holes. "Terrific. I'm supposed to do a death-defying leap today and I can't even dress myself."

She half expected to hear Matt's voice offering to do the job for her. When only silence met her comment,

Chyna decided that he had tired of the game and had gone back to the comforts of his trailer. So when she hurried out of the tent and he stepped out of the shadows, she gasped and jumped back, nearly tripping on a large root.

He reached out in time to steady her. "I thought stuntpeople had nerves of steel," he commented.

"We do," she informed him, trying to shrug away his hands. She had no luck. "When it comes to our own stunts. As for Peeping Toms who leap out of the shadows . . ."

He laughed. "I'm a listening Tom, not a peeping one," he corrected. "And I'd hardly call stepping forward 'leaping.'"

Pulling back, Chyna managed to disentangle herself from his hold. "I don't have time to play word games with you," she said, trying to move past him.

She never made it. "What kind of games *do* you have time for?" he asked, his voice as low and lush as the dark green foliage surrounding them.

"The ones I get paid for—on the set," she added before he had any time to comment on *that*. "I thought producers were supposed to be busy people," she said impatiently.

"We are," he agreed. From the look in his eyes, it was obvious to Chyna that his mind definitely wasn't on the conversation.

"So what are you doing skulking around the showers at three in the morning?" she demanded.

"Waiting for you."

The words vibrated along her skin, raising the tiny hairs along her arm. Still, she tried to keep up the fight. "Why?" There, she had put him on the spot. Or so she hoped.

"Women who talk to themselves fascinate me," he teased.

He was undressing her with his eyes. She could feel it. It made her want to clutch at her clothes. Dummy, he's getting to you. And he was, damn him.

"Do you always talk to yourself?" he asked.

She lifted her chin slightly. "On occasion."

"What kind of occasion?" he prodded.

"On the occasions when sorting things out in my head doesn't quite do the trick," she said curtly. She wished he'd stop probing her this way.

The broad hint wasn't taken.

"So, I'm in your head now, am I?" he asked. Satisfaction was etched into every part of his handsome face.

This wasn't working out right at all. "Why shouldn't you be?" she asked, annoyed. She had walked right into this one. Now she'd have to get herself out. "You're the producer."

His eyes sparkled. He wasn't about to let her off the hook yet. "And do you always think about your producer when you're taking a shower?" The sensuous look in his eyes as they traced the path the water might have taken down her body made her hot despite all her attempts to dismiss his words as just so much empty banter.

Still, she managed to keep the fact that her pulse was racing a secret. "No," she told him, "this is a first. None of my other producers ever stood naked in front of me in a shower stall."

She had hoped to make him feel silly. He didn't. Not if that deep smile on his face was any indication of what was going on inside his head. "I'm glad," he murmured. Round two belonged to him.

Chyna breathed in deeply to buy herself some time. A lungful of stifling air didn't help the situation any. "I've got my stunt to think about today," she announced, trying to get by him again. But as she moved he extended his arm, leaning it against the palm tree to her left. When she turned back his other arm went up, trapping her against the tree. And him. For a moment he looked very serious. And then, quickly, the look was gone.

"You smell good," he observed, lowering his head slightly and letting her wayward golden-brown hair caress his cheek.

"A shower can do wonders," she quipped, struggling not to give in to the sensuous feelings that were starting up in her again. Leave me alone, Matt Harrigan. I need an uncomplicated life. I don't need you in it, not like this. I know what you're up to.

All the logical thoughts in the world couldn't save her.

"No," Matt said softly, dropping the bars of her prison and slipping them around her instead. She felt more trapped than ever. "I think you have a natural perfume about you." The words were said against her neck. Wonderful sensations took wing as his breath stroked her skin. Chyna drew in another lungful of air. It did absolutely no good. She was quickly becoming intoxicated. But she tried again.

Matt looked at her, curious. "Careful," he warned, a smile tugging at the corners of his mouth. "You'll hyperventilate, and I'll have to resort to C.P.R."

Chyna felt her heart hammering against her chest. Here was the famous stuntwoman who leaped over exploding gasoline tanks getting weak-kneed because a man was holding her, she thought cryptically. "You don't give C.P.R. to a person who's hyperventilating," she informed him, her voice husky.

She saw his eyes sweep over the provocative swell of her breasts beneath the half-opened blouse. "I take my opportunities when they come up," he said.

As he spoke, she felt his hands go to either side of her waist, tunneling beneath her open shirttails. His fingers fanned out against her skin. She couldn't move, and her mind went blank. All she could do was watch his eyes. They were like liquid fire, shimmering in the faint rays of dawn. The slow, mesmerizing trail forged by his hands as they traveled upward, stretching, touching, tantalized her. She ached for more.

Chyna could feel her nipples hardening, peaking against the soft material of her bra as they yearned for the touch of a man. This man.

She was crazy. There was no other explanation for this moonlight madness on her part.

"Is there a full moon out?" she asked, her voice nearly lost in the recesses of her growing desire.

"No," he answered without looking up. "In fact, I think the sun's about to come up."

A fraction of a second later the tips of his fingers secured the crests of her breasts, and she gasped in response.

She was a full grown woman who had had a loving, satisfying relationship in her life. So why was the touch of a man who was almost a stranger reducing her to a quivering adolescent? she argued with herself. This had never happened to her before. It shouldn't be happening now, not with a man who was using his sensuality as a weapon to hold her in line. Skin touching skin, that's all it is, she told herself fiercely. But somehow her body wasn't getting the message. It was lost in the message that he was transmitting as his hands cupped her breasts.

It was an extreme effort for her not to gasp as she felt his hands close over her breasts, but she managed to keep silent. What she couldn't control was the look that came over her face as it softened. She was losing the fight, feeling herself slip into the vast, beguiling ocean of passion that was beckoning to her. Its waves lapped at her from all sides.

With slow, deliberate strokes Matt gently massaged her breasts, still leaving them within the cups of her bra. It was as if he were in no hurry, as if he were savoring this as much as she was. He kissed the side of her neck, igniting another rush of desire within her.

This wasn't going to lead to anything except problems, Chyna thought desperately as she tried to break free of the gossamer web of passion that was entangling her. Dragging out her last shred of self-discipline, Chyna pressed her hands against his chest, intent on pushing him back. What she felt stopped her for a moment. Beneath the tips of her fingers she felt the erratic beating of his heart.

It's all a sham, she insisted. He's trained his heart to skip at will. Get away. Now!

Swallowing, Chyna pushed him back to arm's length. "You need a shave," she observed, trying to sound unaffected as she spoke.

"That's not all I need," he whispered, but he didn't try to recapture her in his arms, much to her relief.

"Well, I don't know what else *you* need," Chyna said, avoiding his eyes, "but *I* need to get in a little more practice today if I'm going to pull off that stunt." She began to walk away, but her movements were slow, as if part of her was waiting for him to stop her.

"Chyna?" It was his voice that stopped her. There was something oddly serious about the tone.

"Yes?"

"Be careful." It wasn't an impersonal command. It almost sounded like a plea.

She gave him one more minute before she hurried away. "I always am," she assured him. "Don't worry, Mr. Harrigan. I won't sue if something goes wrong. I intend to check over all the equipment myself. If something happens, it'll be my fault. Besides, if it does, I won't be around to sue," she said cheerfully for what she assumed was his benefit.

To her surprise he didn't return her smile. His expression had turned solemn. "I know that."

His intonation puzzled her all the way back to her shack.

"A hundred and twenty in the shade and we're going to be lighting gasoline tanks," one grip muttered to another as they went about the task of setting up the shot. It had already been postponed twice that day because of unexpectedly capricious wind shifts that affected all Chyna's carefully thought-out calculations.

From where she stood on the mountain, she could see Dussault pacing impatiently. "Happy" was not a word that had applied when the stunt-coordinator had gone to him the first time to say that Chyna wasn't going to attempt the gag until the winds died down. The second time the message was delivered, Dussault had looked as if he had murder on his mind.

That was okay, Chyna thought now. If he was in such an all-fired hurry, *he* could put on a dress and attempt the jump. She wasn't going to do it until everything was just right. She wanted to live to collect her twenty thousand dollars.

Chyna watched, almost unseeing, as the director turned toward the continuity girl and demanded to know if everything in the upcoming shot coordinated with the previous one. The bespectacled older woman nervously went over the checklist on her clipboard and nodded affirmatively.

Dussault turned toward Chyna again. Holding a megaphone to his mouth, he yelled. "Well?"

Chyna looked around. All was still. Cupping her hands around her mouth, she yelled back, "I'm ready."

Dussault dropped his megaphone to the ground and pretended to applaud her. Even from a distance, she couldn't miss his sarcastic intent.

"You mean she's finally ready?"

Chyna turned behind her to look at Sally, who was seated beneath a canopy, fanning herself. She had been sitting there for the better part of two hours, growing increasingly irritated. She was wearing an outfit that was identical to Chyna's. Even the strategically torn parts matched.

"Yes," Chyna answered crisply, " 'she's' ready." She watched the makeup artist spring to life as he began to retouch Sally's makeup, restoring what nature had attempted to destroy with humidity.

"Well, it's about time," Sally said loudly as she shrugged the makeup man aside and moved to the top of the mountain.

Cameras closed in from all angles, recording Sally's touchingly heroic expression just before "she" leaped off the peak.

"Cut!" the assistant director cried. "Wonderful, Sally, wonderful," he enthused, stepping forward and taking the woman's hands in his.

Sure, Chyna thought humorously. Wonderful. All Sally had to do was stand at the top of the mountain. Standing wasn't very hard to do, even for Sally.

"Chyna?" the assistant called, looking over his shoulder toward where she was standing.

Chyna braced herself. Here goes nothing, she thought as she stepped up to the mark that Sally had just toed.

"Ready?" the assistant asked.

For a moment Chyna stood perfectly still, waiting for that inner signal she had come to rely on, the one that told her that it was all right. Yes, everything was ready. She gave a quick nod.

"Ready," she declared.

Out of the corner of her eye she saw the assistant director signal the ground crew below. She heard Dussault roar. "She's finally gonna do it! Roll 'em!"

It had begun.

Earlier, duplicate gasoline tanks had been filmed as they exploded. That was for use with Sally's close-ups. Merging the two shots would be a job for the film editor. Right now, new tanks were exploding, shooting flames in all different directions. Long, bright yellow fingers clawed their way up out of the inferno.

Poetry later, Chyna, she told herself. Jump now. With discipline that had taken her a long time to acquire, Chyna checked out everything in a matter of moments. Concentrating on nothing but hitting that vital spring ramp, she blindly looked over her shoulder at the Nazis who were supposedly chasing the heroine, and took a running leap.

Now!

The pit of her stomach leaped up to meet her throat as she sailed down, totally free, totally unhampered. The intensity of the heat rising up from the exploding tanks was tremendous. She came so close to the flames as she sailed by that she felt her cheeks burning. The reassuring feeling of the spring ramp beneath her feet was one of the most fantastic things she had ever experienced. She came down with such force that she was catapulted back up and over onto the huge air mattress that was waiting to catch her.

A noise that she thought sounded something like "omffp!" came out of her as she sank into the air mattress. She resurfaced only to hear cries of, "Get that damned fire extinguisher!"

The fact that it was Matt's voice registered with her at the same time that she realized she was still the center of a commotion. One bright flame told her why.

She was on fire!

Two seconds later her legs were stinging, surrounded by the cloud of carbon dioxide that came shooting out of the extinguisher. Her dress had caught fire as she had sailed over the flames, but beyond consuming the bottom half of her outfit, the fire had done no damage.

"Did you get it?" she called out the head cameraman, searching him out in the crowd. She certainly didn't want to do that over again.

He gave her the high sign, looking as pleased with the shot as if he had done the jump himself.

Suddenly Chyna felt herself being scooped up by a pair of strong arms, and she saw the look of mingled concern and relief on Matt's face.

Chyna was aware of the fact that she was sooty,

bedraggled, and had definitely been more attractive in the past. "We've got to stop meeting like this," she cracked, breaking the tension for everyone.

"Back to work," Dussault bellowed without so much as one complimentary word tossed in Chyna's direction.

"You're welcome," she muttered audibly.

The bald man shot her an annoyed look. "Thank you," Dussault said sarcastically. "Thank you for earning your pay." He turned his back to her as a new detail took his attention. Chyna looked at Matt to see if Dussault's abrasive behavior had registered with him.

For the moment Matt wasn't interested in Dussault. "Can you walk?" he asked her, still holding her in his arms.

"You ask this of a woman who can fly off mountaintops?" she laughed. "Of course I can walk."

But he didn't set her down. Instead he attempted to walk over to the edge of the mattress so he could hand her down to someone else. All that happened was that he began to totter, and then they both fell onto the air mattress, with Matt landing on top of her.

Despite the fact that she had now disintegrated into peals of laughter over his failed gallantry, Chyna was more than a little aware of the firm imprint his body made on hers.

"Why, Mr. Producer, this is so sudden," she gasped mockingly, placing her hand to her forehead. Laughter punctuated every word.

"Not sudden enough," he said, and the look in his eyes made the laughter die in her throat.

"Need any help, Mr. Harrigan?" the stunt coordinator asked.

Matt's eyes didn't leave Chyna's face. "That remains to be seen," he said quietly, his words for her benefit alone. Before she could make any sort of retort, Matt rolled off her and climbed to the ground. Chyna was prepared to jump down unaided. But as she sailed off the seven foot mattress, Matt caught her in his arms.

"This is getting to be a habit," Chyna observed. She couldn't help smiling. The exhilaration of successfully completing a more than usually dangerous gag was still with her. Everything was perfect. The whole world was perfect, even Dussault and his perpetual frown.

"I certainly hope so," Matt said, but the words didn't sound as glib as she had thought they would, despite the fact that there were several people milling around.

"Are you all right, Mr. Harrigan?" Alex asked solicitously.

Matt looked at him with a touch of amusement. "Why shouldn't I be all right? I just climbed up on the air mattress. She's the one who caught fire," he pointed out, setting Chyna down.

The stunt coordinator grinned. "Great gag, Chyna," he said, clapping her on the back.

As if a signal had gone off, the other stuntworkers all approached, gathering around Chyna. Their voices mingled in hearty congratulation. She barely heard what they were saying; she was trying to keep track of Matt as the crowd grew larger. Their eyes met and held for a long moment, and Chyna was the first to break the contact.

"Well, I've got to get out of this lovely outfit and into a long, cool drink," Chyna said, making her way through the center of the crowd.

"The food trucks are having another refrigeration crisis," Pepper told her, striking a death knell over her hopes of refreshment.

"Aren't we all?" Chyna sighed. She wiped away a bead of perspiration that had followed a zigzag pattern from her temple down her cheek.

"My refrigeration's working," Matt offered.

And so is everything else that belongs to you, Chyna thought. Which is why I'm staying clear of you.

"No," Chyna said, shaking her head as the others went on about their work, leaving them standing alone. "I've decided to opt for just a shower."

"Need any help?" he asked, and then he smiled before she could answer. "No, I guess not. Anyone as capable as you are doesn't need any help."

Was she mistaken, or was there a hint of admiration in his voice?

"No," she heard herself murmur. "I don't need any help." With that she walked away, but she felt him watching her every step.

7

It was all well and good to tell herself that she wouldn't fall into his trap when she wasn't around him. But one look into his shimmering green eyes and she felt herself losing ground. So the most sensible thing, Chyna decided, was to stay far away from Matt.

That, however, proved to be impossible.

The next day's shooting schedule involved another gag, one she had nothing to do with, but she watched nonetheless. What she saw was a near-fatal accident involving a runaway car and a cameraman positioned too close to the scene for his own safety. During the commotion that followed the incident, Chyna turned toward Alex. He read her mind instantly.

"Nothing happened, Chyna," he said between gritted teeth.

This time, she thought angrily, watching him placate the head cameraman. The loud hum of mingled voices began to subside as Chyna walked away from the scene. Alex would never stand up for them, she thought, the fact bothering her twice as much because of their past friendship. She stopped walking for a moment, looking in the direction of Matt's trailer. He had told her to come to him with her grievances. She had felt at the time that he was only trying to mollify her, and nothing had happened to change her mind. But it was worth a shot. She had nothing to lose.

Her palms began to sweat as she raised her hand to knock on his door.

"C'mon in," she heard Matt call out. "The door's open."

He didn't sound very friendly, she thought. As a matter of fact, he sounded rather tired. This probably wasn't going to be the best time to approach him with a problem. But then, when would? She pulled back her shoulders and walked in.

She found him sitting bare chested at the desk, scowling. He didn't look up at first. Something was bothering him, and she couldn't help wondering what.

When he didn't hear anything, Matt looked up and saw Chyna studying him. He looked mildly surprised to see her. "To what do I owe this pleasure?" he asked. "Need another shirt?"

His scowl faded into a rather sad expression, even though he smiled at her, and Chyna felt something tug at her heart. As she moved forward she realized that he was holding his daughter's picture.

"Something wrong?" she felt compelled to ask.

A bemused smile met her question. "You came in to find out if something was wrong? I didn't know I frowned so loudly."

"Certain noises carry out here," she answered

drolly. "Dussault's scowls make the trees shake. He . . ." But she let her voice slip away for a moment. Suddenly she didn't want to talk about Dussault. Not just now. Something was bothering Matt, and she wanted to know what it was. In that moment Chyna realized that Matt *had* succeeded in at least part of his plan to keep her quiet. She was intimately involved with him despite the fact that they had done little more than kiss. There was something about him that stirred her, and it wasn't just physical. Maybe it had something to do with the fact that he had been the first at her side when she had caught fire. Whatever it was, she knew she cared about him, cared about what made him unhappy. She was going to have to watch her step to make sure that he didn't use her feelings against her.

Leaning across the desk, Chyna nodded toward the picture. "Is it about your daughter?" she pressed.

His eyes shifted from her face down to the photograph he was holding. He put it back in its place. "It's her birthday," he told Chyna.

"And you forgot it," she said. Typical man, she thought affectionately. Still, he did look disappointed.

"No, it's next week," he answered.

"Oh." She was at a loss as to why he looked so crestfallen. "Didn't you expect her to have one this year?" she asked, seeking recourse in a lighter tone.

"Not without me," he replied, his voice just the slightest bit annoyed.

She felt another tug at her heart as she realized that being separated from his daughter really bothered him. It made him seem more real to her, more human. She felt herself losing even more ground.

"Always been with her before?" she asked softly. Just like her own father, she thought, when she was younger. He had always been there for her.

"Always," he answered, trying to sound brisk.

"Then why don't you fly out?" she urged. It seemed a simple enough solution, she thought.

But he shook his head. "Can't," he told her, pushing back his chair and getting up. He sighed. "I'm needed here. There's too much to do."

"That's what assistants are for," she pointed out.

"I did that once," he told her. He leveled his gaze at her face. "I think you'll remember the name of the picture."

He was talking about Neil's picture, she suddenly realized. Was he trying to explain away his part in it? Or make her believe that it had all been a mistake? She knew that. She knew he hadn't willfully tried to cause anyone an injury—or worse. Negligence was all she had ever charged him with. She tried to interpret the somber expression in his eyes. Did he feel responsible for the accident? Chyna pushed the thought away, not wanting to go over the past anymore.

She cleared her throat. "I wanted to talk to you about Dussault . . ." she began. And I wish you'd stop standing so close to me, she added silently. But she made no effort to back away herself.

"What about him?" he asked patiently.

"He's displaying a flagrant disregard for people's safety. This morning I saw a cameraman practically mowed down by an out-of-control car. If Dussault hadn't been so anxious to get the shot in one take, he would have let the man stand in a safer spot." *She* should be standing in a safer spot, she told herself, her thoughts drifting from the subject at hand. Being so close to him made her want him, made her long for things that had absolutely no place in this discussion. Her next words were said in a rush as she tried to beat back her feelings. "We also need a new insert car."

Her statement threw him. "What's wrong with the old one?" he asked evenly.

"Nothing, if you like having death as your co-pilot," she answered. "Dussault has them driving that thing at breakneck speed, and its center of gravity is far too high. I saw them careening around in it this morning. One of these days it's going to flip over when it's making a turn." The sobering words helped her quell some of the fire she felt inside. "There's a new prototype out," she went on. "It has *every* safety feature imaginable. Most insert cars are just stripped down pickups with some equipment loaded on. That's fine if you're a gardener on your way to mulch a lawn. It's not too terrific when you're practically flying around, trying to capture a wild chase scene."

He considered her words for a moment, but then he shook his head and her hopes dimmed. "Do you have any idea how much a new insert car would cost?" he asked her.

"A lot less than a man's life," she answered firmly. "Can you stand to have two lives on your conscience?" she asked, the words pouring out before she could stop them. Instantly she was sorry.

She saw the muscles of his jawline tighten slightly, and knew then that she had hit below the belt. He *did* feel responsible for what had happened. Whatever else he was doing now by trying to keep her away from Dussault, he did hold himself responsible for what had happened to Neil.

"I'm sorry," she said, her voice dropping.

"So am I," he told her. "I'll see what I can do."

With his softened words, the scene had turned intimate; something was pulling her toward him. This was just what he wanted, she thought. And yes, it was just what she wanted, too, heaven help her. She felt so drawn to him that it was almost painful.

"Well, that solves my problem," she said, her voice sounding stilted as she tried vainly to curtail the emotions she felt. "Now, what about yours?" she prodded.

His eyes made her think of a green flame. "I'm looking at it," he whispered, bending his head toward her.

If he kissed her now, she would be done for. As he put his arms around her shoulders, she pressed her hands against his chest. She meant to block his move. Instead she curled her hands along the sensuous, hard lines formed by his pectorals. The lure of his body grew.

"No," she said, her voice increasingly unsteady. "I meant your daughter."

He kissed her hair. "What about her?"

"If you can't go there, why don't you fly her out here for her birthday?" Chyna urged, her senses beginning to spin. Fine stuntwoman you are, she thought, getting dizzy just standing still.

Matt rolled the idea over in his mind. "Here?" he echoed, holding her back as he looked down into her face.

"Here," she repeated. His surprised expression amused her a little. "Have you been suffering from this hearing deficiency long?"

"I've been suffering from a lot of things since you

turned up," he told her softly, the words caressing her. "But I can't fly Meredith out here. She's only five—"

"She won't have to fly the plane, just sit in it," Chyna teased, feeling very close to him, emotionally as well as physically. She turned serious for a moment, setting aside her flippant humor as she thought of the girl in the picture. "Have someone come out with her. She'll appreciate the fact that her daddy thought enough of her to send for her. Nothing's worse than spending your birthday with strangers, no matter how well they're paid to take care of you." She put her hand on his arm. "You're going to be a busy man for the rest of your life," she pointed out, wondering how she was managing to make intelligent conversation when her insides had been reduced to the consistency of cotton candy. "You don't want Meredith to look at you in eighteen years and say, 'Hi, Stranger,' when you walk through the door, right?"

"Good point," he conceded. The space that existed between them shrank to nothing as he pulled her close again. "I've been noticing lately that you have a lot of good points," he murmured, his lips finally covering hers.

There was no way she was leaving. She knew that. He had successfully broken down every single defense at her disposal. She wanted him. Whatever his motives, whatever his reasons for bringing her to this moment, she wanted him. Every fiber in her body cried out for fulfillment. Being so close to him, having his body move lightly against hers, was sheer torture.

But some shred of pride forced her to at least try to make an excuse, to try to leave just one more time. When his lips temporarily moved to assault her neck,

Chyna said breathily, "I've got . . . to . . . practice . . ."

She felt his hands beneath her bustline, tenderly
caressing the aching fullness of her breasts. His strokes
echoed the rhythm of her breathing.

"You don't need any practice," he whispered, the
words curling into the hollow of her throat just as his
lips touched her. "I have a feeling you're letter
perfect."

Slowly he encircled her throat with a ring of burning
kisses. She was vaguely aware of the fact that he was
now behind her, taking possession of the base of her
neck. An army of throbbing sensation marched up and
down her spine in answer to the machinations of his
tongue.

"This tie is getting in my way," Chyna heard him
say, half-teasing, half-serious.

"How . . . do you . . . generally . . . deal with . . .
something that . . . gets in . . . your . . . way?" she
asked haltingly, delicious sensations racing through
her body.

"Usually," he said, his words hot against her neck,
"I try to reason with it."

Or seduce it, she thought, receding into a misty
haze. There was no turning back. No lifeline to grasp.
She knew she wouldn't clutch at it even if one existed.

"But I don't think reason has any place here," he
was saying. His words were separated by tiny, butter-
flylike kisses that captured her soul as soon as they
touched her neck.

So, you're seducing it, just like you're seducing me,
she thought, her eyelids getting heavy. She closed her
eyes, savoring every scrap of emotion that she was
experiencing. She was struck by the wonder of it. Fire

and passion mingled in her veins, though so little had actually happened. What kind of an effect did this man have on her? Her head continued to spin.

The kisses stopped, and she felt the tie that held secure her halter top loosen. From the feel of his breath along the slope of her neck, he was undoing the tie with his teeth. She tried to stop a shiver from going through her at the same time that she felt her knees begin to weaken.

Chyna felt the front of her pink halter top begin to sag, but still he didn't turn her around. Instead Matt just held her against his chest, massaging her breasts and gently rubbing the palms of his hands against her nipples. Erratic signals made their way to her brain, foretelling both ecstasy and danger. She chose to ignore the second message. She had no choice, actually. All this had been preordained. She could feel it. It was almost as if her body were on automatic pilot. But he couldn't think that it was going to be so easy, her mind pleaded.

"Matt, I . . . don't think . . ."

"Good," he said, his lips meeting the rounded edge of her shoulder. It began to glow with his warmth. "Thinking's bad for you. Bad for us."

"Us?" she breathed. How could one word sound so lovely? Especially when she knew it wasn't true.

Matt turned her around. As he did so the fabric of her top slipped down further, hanging precariously across the hardened peaks of her nipples, displaying the swell of her breasts to his hungry gaze.

She saw the look in his eyes and feasted on it. It nurtured her own smoldering desire.

"Us," he repeated. "That signifies the presence of more than one person in a situation."

"Is that what this is?" she asked, her throat incredibly dry. This time she couldn't blame it on the weather. The air conditioning in the room was giving her goose bumps. Who was she kidding? He was giving her goose bumps.

Slowly he ran his finger along her lips. "What?"

"A situation," she repeated.

"I certainly hope so."

Pressing his hand against the curve of her waist, he tugged on her top until it fell to her waist like the flag of a defeated country.

"Beautiful," he said, drinking in the sight before him.

Chyna was tempted to cover her breasts, but he was there before her, cupping them like long-sought-for treasures that had finally been attained. Chills ran all through her, clearing the way for another wave of molten fire. She had to press her lips together to keep a moan from escaping.

"I have to . . . go." But her body gave the lie to her words as she arched herself against his touch. His hands were stroking her, raising the fever within her higher and higher.

He lowered his head. Warm lips touched silken flesh. This time, the moan did escape. "No," he murmured, "you don't *have* to do anything." Raising his head again, he tilted hers back until their eyes met. "Not even stay here."

First he drove her out of her mind, then he told her that she was free to go. Free? She was no more free to walk away than a deep sea diver was free to strip himself of his oxygen tanks and swim away. Right now, he was her lifeline. What he had to offer her was more dear than the very air she breathed.

"You're making this very difficult," she complained, some of her senses returning to her—but diminishing none of her passion. "How can I tell myself you seduced me if you're giving me a way out?"

The smile she received made her heart beat faster with joy. Taking her face between his hands, Matt kissed her almost fiercely. She tasted all the passion, all the desire, that the smile had hidden from her. He wanted her. He wanted her as much as she wanted him. The realization increased the intense excitement she felt.

"We'll come up with some excuse for your conscience later," he promised, his smile answering the one that was growing on her own lips.

"Are you very good at excuses?" she asked as he picked her up in his arms. She put one of her own arms around his neck, cradling herself against the warmth of his chest. What excuse would he give her later? After this interlude was over and he wanted to go back to life as usual . . . back to business as usual.

"Yes," he answered honestly, carrying her into his tiny bedroom. From her vantage point, it looked like all bed and nothing else. But that was what she wanted right now—an endless bed where she could give herself up to the pleasures of loving him. "But I'm better at other things," he told her. It was a whispered promise.

She felt his velveteen bedspread against her bare back. It felt sultry, like his voice. She saw nothing but him as he filled the room with his presence. The yearning within her feathered out to every corner of her being. "What things?" she asked, her voice low.

He came to her on the bed, the length of his body touching hers. "Has anyone ever told you that you talk too much?" he asked, his hands tracing the valleys of her seminude body.

"Yes."

"Good, then it's not just me."

"Yes, it is," Chyna whispered, knowing her voice would crack if she spoke any louder. "Just you." He was making everything within her vibrate, playing her like a fine musical instrument, producing a melody from within her that she had never known herself capable of. The fierceness of her desire both surprised and excited her.

Matt seemed to understand the meaning behind her simple words and he pulled her to him, his eyes burning into hers. She saw the incredible amount of controlled hunger there, and her breathing became shallow even before his lips met hers. Over and over again, his mouth slanted against hers, draining her of her very essence, taking everything from her and yet giving her something wonderful back in return. She felt more alive, more exhilarated, than she ever had before. It was as if she were building up to the longest chuteless jump of her career. His kisses had the same dizzying effect. They created the same whirling anticipation in her stomach.

Vaguely the fact that there was material sliding down along her thigh penetrated her consciousness.

"Lift, please." The sensual command caressed her ear.

"Hmm?"

"I'm trying to undress you," Matt said. "I need a little help."

Chyna opened her eyes, trying to pull the world into focus. He was the only thing she could focus on. She raised her hips slightly.

"Like I said when I met you," she breathed. "I don't make waves."

"Oh, but you have. You have," he told her. His voice sounded tight, as if he were struggling not to reveal the emotions that were building inside him.

With long, caressing motions, he removed her white shorts and the tiny bit of lace that served as her underwear. She heard his sharp intake of breath.

Hold me. Love me, she wanted to cry out. But the words stuck in her throat as she watched him watching her. He was a portrait of restraint, and she was fast becoming a quivering mess. She wasn't sure if she could bear his sweeping touch any longer. There was just so much stoking that a fire could take before it rampaged out of control.

"Are you always this slow?" she murmured, trying to keep from sounding impatient.

"Thorough," he corrected. "The word is thorough. I want to savor every bit of you." But as he began to kiss her again, Chyna forced him back. If he was going to tantalize her, then she was going to give him back as good as she got.

"If you're so 'thorough,' how come you forgot to take off your own clothes?" she asked.

She saw the twinkle enter his eyes. "Why don't you do the honors?" he suggested. His teasing tone was back, even though she felt his heart hammering against her hand, which still rested on his chest.

She cocked her head, her hair fanning out against his pillow. "Is that a dare?"

He knew he had her then. "Can't resist one, can you?" he asked, rolling onto his back. He laced his fingers together beneath his head and watched her face, waiting.

He was right. More than that, she couldn't resist him. She wanted to shred the barriers between them with eager hands. Instead, she sat up and rocked back on her heels, slowly taking his belt into her hand and uncinching it. A gleam came into his eyes as she released the catch at the top of his trousers. Watching his face for every telltale nuance, Chyna slowly drew the zipper down. She felt him move against her ever so slightly as a flush came into his cheeks. Good. Let him feel what she was feeling. Let him burn the way she was burning.

"Don't stop now," he urged thickly when she paused. "You're coming to the best part."

"For whom?" she asked, wishing she didn't sound so breathless, wishing she could look as controlled as he did.

"For both of us," he answered.

He took her hands and placed them on either side of his muscular hips. Bracing his feet against the bed, he raised himself just enough for Chyna to finish what she had started. She didn't even see or hear the trousers hit the floor. She was too busy reveling in the new emotions that flooded through her as Matt pressed her hands against his hot flesh.

"One more article," he whispered.

Her bold mood left, but it was too late for her to back down, too late to run for cover.

They shed the last barrier together. She didn't even know if his hands were guiding hers, or if she had taken the lead again.

"Come here, Chyna," he called softly, opening his arms to her.

Gone was the woman who had wanted him to come to her. Gone was the woman who had wanted to teach him a lesson. She had been replaced by a woman who only wanted to be loved. Loved by this man alone. Later there would be time enough to worry about the consequences of her actions. Later she would plot a way out of her dilemma and make him love her. Right now was the time to abandon herself to the ecstasy that beckoned.

She felt his hands on her hips as he pulled her toward him, pressing her flesh against his. The fire roared, spreading its magic through her veins, igniting every part of her. This time there was no safety crew around to put it out. This was the most dangerous stunt of her career.

And she loved it.

8

~00000000000~

She had no power to stop what was happening, nor any desire to. What she was feeling had the momentum of a jet and it was whisking her away into heaven, a heaven she had never dreamed of before.

When Matt shifted his weight and entered her, it was the most divine sensation she had ever experienced. As the depth of his kisses increased, Chyna closed her eyes and wound her fingers into his thick hair, wanting to pull him closer to her, wanting to absorb every sparkling emotion that he was awakening within her. Wanting to absorb him. Forever.

Dear Lord, did it happen like this? Did love just burst upon you? The only other time she had fallen in love, it had happened gradually, like the long-awaited blooming of a spring flower, not like an exploding gasoline tank. Yet here it was, exploding all around her, engulfing her. And she couldn't do a thing about it.

She couldn't even think anymore, only feel. And what she felt was ecstasy.

Chyna opened her eyes to find Matt looking down at her. Part of her had been afraid of this moment, afraid that she would read triumph in his gaze, as if he had succeeded in his carefully planned conquest.

But there was no triumph on his face, only a very tender smile. She rallied slightly, even though she told herself not to rejoice just yet. After all, maybe he was just winding down from lovemaking. She wasn't exactly versed in what men looked like after they made love to a woman.

His smile was beautiful. *He* was beautiful. Steady, the game isn't over yet, Chyna. Now you have to be more cautious than ever. Now he knows your weaknesses.

He brushed her hair away from her face. When had she ever felt a gesture so incredibly gentle? "This might open up a whole new avenue of negotiations between producers and stuntpeople," he said softly, his eyes teasing her.

He had meant it as a joke, but Chyna stiffened, afraid of what he might be thinking. "I don't barter that way," she said, her tone deadly calm.

"I know."

And somehow she knew he did. She knew that he had learned more about her in this brief interlude than other people had in a lifetime.

She propped herself up on one elbow, a grin on her face. "But since you brought it up—what about the insert car?" she asked.

Matt began to laugh. It was a low, pleasure-filled laugh that was replaced by a broad smile as he pulled her closer to him. "You remind me a lot of my father," he told her.

What an odd thing to say. But then, asking about an insert car after a passionate session of lovemaking wasn't exactly normal, either.

"Why?" she asked, curling up against him. "Did he ask you for an insert car, too?"

Matt began to slide his hand along the curve of her body, his gentle caresses arousing her again. She could feel the smoldering fires reigniting in her veins. "No, but he had the same kind of bulldog stick-to-itiveness that you seem to display."

"Sounds like a wonderful man," she commented. "What's he doing these days?" Did he hear the catch in her throat as his hand dipped lower? Breathing normally was getting to be very, very difficult around him.

"Not much of anything. He died five years ago."

"Oh."

His answer surprised her and momentarily freed her from the effect of his touch. "I'm sorry. Do you miss him?" she asked, peering up at his face. She was sure she had detected a great deal of fondness in his voice when he had mentioned his father.

He laid her flat on the bed, pinning her down with the weight of his chest. "Not right now."

"No, I mean really," she pressed, wanting to know about him. She suddenly felt a great desire to find out more about this man who aroused such inexplicably wonderful feelings inside her.

He sighed a little, and she could see a different, faraway look enter his eyes. "He was a terrific old man," Matt said. "Gruff, feisty. I thought the world of him."

And he said I reminded him of his father, she thought. The thought warmed her.

"Yes," Matt went on, looking down into her face, "I miss him. Any other questions?" he asked, a grin tugging at his lips.

"Yes, just one."

"Which is?" His forefinger curled along her cheek as he traced a slow path to her lower lip.

"When are you going to make love to me again?" she asked, her voice husky. She made no effort to hide her desire.

"Demands," he murmured, covering her mouth with his own. "Always demands."

Her demands were met beyond her wildest dreams.

"They're going to be wondering where you are," Chyna said as she lay in bed, cradled in his arms. Her tousled head rested against him, and she could feel the rhythmic movement of his chest as he breathed. The tiny hairs caressed her cheek. A warm glow still burned inside her, a warm glow she tried to hang on to, knowing it would be gone all too soon. The euphoria created by his lovemaking hadn't blotted out the words she had heard him say to Dussault.

Could someone make love like that and not feel anything? She knew she couldn't. But could he? Did he mean to hold her in check with chains forged of love? She told herself it wouldn't work, but there was a small kernel of doubt forming even now.

"I'm in heaven," Matt answered, making no movement to get up.

Chyna looked around the tiny bedroom. "Heaven's kind of cramped," she observed dryly.

He bent his head to kiss the top of hers. "That's what makes it heaven."

She glanced down at her watch. "It's four o'clock," she prodded. Part of her wanted to disentangle herself from him, literally and otherwise. But part of her wanted to stay, fearing that this joy could never be recaptured again, and she wanted to hang on to the blissful feelings just a little while longer. Even now they were fading away as reality impinged on the private world she and Matt had made.

"I didn't know they had a clock in heaven," he commented. She felt his chest rise and fall with a sigh. "But I suppose you're right. There are things I'm supposed to be looking into."

"Like the insert car?" Chyna laughingly reminded him, sitting up and looking around for her clothes.

"Like the insert car," he repeated, shaking his head in disbelief. "You never give up, do you?" he asked.

She had just put on her underwear, and she turned to look at him; she was a magnificent specimen of womanhood done up in a bit of lace. "No."

He had never thought that he could care for a woman who was wound up in her career, but Matt found himself admiring her spirited, independent quality. He liked the way she wouldn't back down. There were a lot of things he liked about her, this woman who had been all set to drag him into court a little less than a year ago. Life was full of funny twists, he thought.

She could see him fighting an urge to take her back into his arms. Maybe two could play at this game, she thought. Maybe she could turn the tables on him and make him as emotionally tied to her as she suspected he wanted her to be to him. Would their plans cancel each other out? Or would they give birth to something twice as strong? Her thoughts were getting jumbled, and she pushed them aside. Get dressed first, she told herself. One thing at a time.

"Yup," he said. She could see him retreating to his glib, easy-going mood. "Just like my father. We had a lot of arguments, too," he said casually.

Too? Were they having an argument?

"Who won?" she asked, reaching behind her back to tie her top.

He came up behind her, wearing only his slacks, and took the ties from her hands. She liked the feel of his fingers as they brushed against her back. "I plead the fifth," Matt said, turning her around to face him.

"Then there's hope," she said with a smile.

His eyes seemed to be searching for something, some sign in her face. It made her wonder. "I've discovered that there's always hope," he told her just before he kissed her.

She could feel the gossamer web beginning to rise around her again. If she weren't careful, it would grow strong enough to trap her. Was there no end to the passion he could generate in her? By all rights she should be an exhausted rag doll. And he . . . well, he should have been laid up for at least a day. But here he was, doing those magical things to her again.

Chyna wedged her hands against his bare chest. "You're incredible," she informed him, a bemused grin underscoring her words.

He rested his hands on her hips. "I've been told that once or twice," he teased.

"By adoring women," she concluded, attempting to appear nonchalant.

"I don't know," he said. "Are you an adoring woman?"

The question was far too probing. He was quick, she'd give him that. "I'm a woman in a hurry. I still have to practice," she said, breaking away. She walked back into the main living area. It was like stepping out of Wonderland into the real world.

See, Chyna, nothing's changed. His desk is still a mess. The sun is still streaming in through the window. Nothing's changed, she insisted.

But she knew she was wrong. Something had been irreversibly changed inside of her.

She reached the door before he could come up behind her. "I still say you don't have to practice," Matt said to her back. "What I found was absolutely perfect."

"Always room for improvement," she shot back gaily just before she left.

It would have been nice to get a lungful of invigorating air when she stepped out of his trailer, but none was available. The humid atmosphere made her want to turn around and march right back in. A lot of things made her want to turn around and march right back in. A lot of other things propelled her in the opposite direction. She was determined to get things under control before she faced him again.

"This woman's life is coming off like the *Perils of Pauline*," Chyna muttered the next day as she took Matt's hand and got up from the ground. Her clothes were charred, despite having been thoroughly soaked with fire retardant chemicals. The heroine had caught on fire while fleeing a burning building.

A grip handed her a towel. As Chyna began wiping the soot off herself, she noticed a strange look on Matt's face.

"What's the matter?" she asked.

Behind them, Sally was preparing to take Chyna's place. Her melodic voice was raised, complaining about having soot applied to her perfect features. Chyna smiled wryly, wondering what the woman would be saying if she had had to earn the dirty marks the way Chyna had just done.

But Sally occupied Chyna's attention only fleetingly, and then Chyna looked toward Matt and waited for an answer to her question.

"I've never watched someone I care for get set on fire before," he said simply. "It takes some getting used to."

"You should try it from this side," she cracked, draping the towel around her neck and letting it soak up the layer of perspiration that had formed there. Unconsciously she tensely gripped the two ends in her hands. He had used the words "care for." Well, what did she expect him to say? This was all part of his plan, wasn't it? He was a good-looking, intelligent man. He knew that one exciting afternoon of love wasn't going to render her permanently docile. His was a long range game plan that would require his participation until the picture was wrapped up.

But her logic still didn't prevent her from feeling a tingle of excitement at the words. He was turning her body against her, she thought in semidespair.

"No thanks," Matt said, turning down her "offer." "I don't have a death wish."

"Neither do I," Chyna said, turning serious. "Why are you so down on stuntwork?" she asked.

"I'm not down on stuntwork," he told her mildly. "I'm down on *you* doing stuntwork, I guess."

How honest he sounded, she thought. She could almost believe him. Almost. "Oh?" she prodded, wondering how far he would go. "Tell me more."

He took hold of her arm, pulling her away from the steady stream of grips and extras who were milling around, waiting for the next scene to begin. "Damn it, Chyna," he said, lowering his voice. It sounded all the more intense that way. "You're the first *real* woman in my life. I don't intend to lose you to some freak accident."

"Fine," she said, trying to keep the tremor out of her voice. He was acting. Only acting, she insisted. "Then keep the freak accidents from happening."

"I'm not God, Chyna," he said, looking somewhat annoyed.

"No, but you could do a few Godlike things," she pointed out. She was about to enumerate them when he cut in.

"I thought I already had," he said, his tone and mood shifting abruptly.

"O ye of little modesty, spare me." Chyna laughed despite the serious nature of the conversation.

"I don't intend to," Matt told her. She couldn't make heads or tails of the expression on his face.

He's just trying to confuse you, she told herself. See, he's turning the conversation away from your subject.

"What about getting the insert car?" she asked, doggedly refusing to let him get away with his evasive tactics.

"I haven't looked into it yet," he said simply.

Well, at least he hadn't tried to lie and tell her it was

on its way, she thought. "Why not?" she asked, knowing that she was putting him on the spot. Better him than someone's life.

"In case you haven't noticed, there aren't any phones out here," he said patiently. As he spoke he took her towel and trailed one end across her breast, managing to brush his fingertips against the high swell.

Chyna took a step back. She wasn't about to let him fog up her brain again. "But there are in Metro Manila," she countered. "I hear it's a nice place to visit."

With that she decided to let the subject drop. She couldn't very well engage him in verbal combat right here in front of everyone. And she had more than a sneaking suspicion that if she got him alone right then, they wouldn't wind up discussing insert cars.

Chyna hurried off to her shack.

She had hardly had enough time to wash her hair and put on clean clothes when a knock sounded on the door. She swung it open. Her visitor was Matt.

"Coming?" he asked.

She looked behind him and saw a Jeep. "Coming where?" she asked, bewildered.

"To Metro Manila. After all, it was your idea," he said brightly.

"What?" She felt as if they were engaged in two different conversations. This man had the ability to muddle her thinking processes more than anyone or anything she had ever come up against.

"You said Metro Manila was a nice place to visit, so I intend to visit it. But I hate making trips alone."

"I'll bet," she quipped, but a smile was already forming on her lips. He was irresistible.

"So, will you come?" he asked.

"How can I say no to the producer?" she asked. Quickly she picked up her purse and took his arm.

"I'll keep that in mind," Matt said, putting his hand against the small of her back and guiding her to the waiting Jeep.

Metro Manila, Chyna found, was a bright collage of old and new, mostly new. The deeper into the city they drove, the more modern the surroundings became.

"I feel like we've just gone through a time warp. This looks just like Los Angeles," Chyna commented, absorbing the atmosphere. "Except that it's cleaner."

Matt grinned at her remark. "They haven't had as much time to litter it as we have. Damn."

"What's the matter?" she asked, looking around to find the cause of his irritation.

"I just missed the turn," he said, nodding off to the right.

"You sure you know how to get to wherever it is we're going?" she asked hesitantly, although the prospect of getting lost with Matt for the day *did* have its appeal.

"I'll have you know that I have wonderful homing instincts," he told her, taking a turn on the next block.

"Seems to me you must have left them home."

"You can dispense with the wry commentary— unless, of course, you'd rather walk." He cast a mischievous glance her way.

Chyna raised her hands as she sank down into her seat. "I surrender. I'll be good."

"I know you will," he murmured under his breath.

Now just what did he mean by that? she wondered, almost afraid of the answer.

The steady flow of traffic eventually brought them back to the previous block. Matt stopped the Jeep before an imposing-looking hotel. The Manila Hilton, the fancy lettering on the awning proclaimed.

"What are we doing here?" Chyna asked.

"I have a room reserved here," he told her, taking her hand and leading her inside. Chyna stopped short, throwing him off balance just shy of the revolving door.

"I didn't come for a tour of your room," she told him.

"It's not that big a room," he said with a laugh, leading her through the regular door next to the revolving one. "But it does have a phone in it. You know, like the ones they use to make calls back to the States with."

She pressed her lips together as she followed him into the lobby. He was laughing at her. "Does that mean you're going to call about the insert car?" she demanded.

"Could be."

He was being so evasive, yet his words were the only thing she had to go on. She was no longer sure if he were just playing games or if she were beginning to wear him down. He was certainly beginning to wear *her* down. There was no question of that in her mind. He wasn't even touching her, and already she could feel herself responding to him, tantalized by the prospect of being alone with him in a hotel room.

And what a hotel room. The lobby was tastefully ornate, with gold carpets and plush chairs alternating with strategically placed marble statues. But the room itself made her think of something out of a magazine. It wasn't a room, it was a suite, with cream-colored walls

115

accented by deep brown molding. The carpet was lush and brown, tempting her to kick off her sandals, which she did as she waited for Matt to finish his phone call.

As she watched him at the white French provincial desk, she tried not to let her thoughts wander in the direction they had seemed to favor ever since he had come into her life. It did no good to try to reason with herself, though. She knew what she was hoping for.

He's drawn you away from the set. He's done what he promised Dussault he'd do. And he's planning to enjoy himself in the process. Why are you being such a fool? She asked herself.

She had no answers, only churning feelings.

She wandered over to the window and looked at the bustling crowds outside. Who would ever have thought, a year ago, that she would be here, thousands of miles away from home, in a hotel room with Matt Harrigan, aching for him to love her again? Life was very, very strange.

"Yes, yes, I know it's short notice, Wanda."

Chyna turned back to him as his conversation floated into her consciousness.

"Wanda?" she echoed.

He covered the receiver. "My unflappable housekeeper," he explained. "There's nothing to be afraid of, Wanda," he said, returning to his conversation. "Flying is safer than driving—especially the way you drive. Now, I want Meredith here on her birthday. . . ."

The negotiations took a full ten minutes, but finally Matt managed to convince Wanda to come with the child in tow.

"Sounds like your unflappable housekeeper was

doing a little flapping there," Chyna commented when he hung up.

"She hates to fly," he said with a shrug, sitting on the desktop. "Doesn't even like riding on ferris wheels."

"Sounds like a real daredevil," she quipped. "Well, what about your other phone call?" she asked, playing with the telephone cord.

"Oh, yes, that one," he said.

"Yes, *that* one." She wondered if he were going to come up with an excuse at the last minute, then try to throw her off guard by making love to her again. The thought sent shivers running along her spine.

Surprisingly, he said nothing at all. Instead he started dialing again. This conversation took a lot longer and didn't have the same result as the first one had. He came up empty.

"What happened?" she asked as he replaced the phone in its cradle.

"No dice," he told her. "They said they couldn't send one out. Too impractical, too expensive and too little time. They'll try to have one ready when we get back to the studio." He sighed and shrugged. "It's the best I can do."

Was it? she wondered. Had he even called the studio at all? For all she knew he could have placed a long distance call to the time lady and carried on his end of the discussion while a recording quoted the time to him every ten seconds.

"Well, you tried," Chyna answered, her voice a little stiff. What was she supposed to believe? Which inner instincts was she supposed to go with?"

He slipped his arms around her waist. "Yes, I did."

She took hold of his arms as he held her from

behind, and with a tug that surprised him, she pulled them away. "And you're trying again," she chided playfully. "But I said I'd heard that Metro Manila was a nice place to visit, remember?" she said. "So let's visit it," she urged.

But as she walked briskly past him, he surprised her by catching her wrist in his hand. It wasn't a hard grip. On the contrary, it was gentle, and it held her more securely for that very reason.

"I know a better place to visit," he said softly.

"Oh?" she asked, her voice higher than usual. "Where?"

"This room right here—with you."

9

—◦◦◦◦◦◦◦◦◦◦—

Sorry, I'm not on the tourist map," she said, trying to sound blasé.

"I like things that are off the beaten path," he whispered, touching her hair.

Still she resisted. Or tried to. "You're going to love the volcano," she told him, turning with her wrist still in his hand and then leading him toward the door.

He laughed, going along with her. "I think I already do."

Was he trying to imply what she thought he was implying? All this inner conflict was beginning to really get to her. Just have a nice time, she told herself. Analyze it later.

But as he closed the hotel room door behind them, she felt just the slightest tinge of regret. She was definitely confused, she thought as they took the elevator back down to the ground floor.

The street outside the hotel was overflowing with

119

people—tourists and natives alike. What caught Chyna's eye as they made their way to the Jeep were the street vendors with their carts of "untold treasures." They made quite a contrast to the executive types who were hurrying off to grab a cocktail or two at the end of the day.

"Bracelet, pretty lady?"

Chyna turned around to find a gnarled old woman tugging at her sleeve. She was holding up a green, wooden bracelet. Tiny mirrors were embedded around its perimeter, reflecting light in all directions.

"She looks like the wicked witch straight out of 'Snow White and The Seven Dwarfs,' doesn't she?" Chyna asked Matt, lowering her voice.

Matt was just about to get into the Jeep when he turned to look at the stoop-shouldered old woman. "I'd be careful if I were you, then." He chuckled, humoring Chyna. "The bracelet might be poisoned."

"If I remember my fairy tales correctly, it was a poisoned comb she tucked into Snow White's hair. And she fed her a poisoned apple. Poisoned jewelry was more Lucretia Borgia's territory."

"I love a well-read woman," Matt said, taking hold of Chyna's arm and trying to usher her into the Jeep.

But Chyna wasn't ready to go just yet. "Matt, she looks like she could use the money," she insisted in a hushed whisper.

"So do a lot of other street vendors," he told her. "They're probably richer than you and I put together." But he saw Chyna's determination, so he released her arm and reluctantly followed, waiting patiently as she began to browse through the jumbled paraphernalia in the chipped wooden cart.

The woman smiled widely. "Want something, pretty lady?" she asked.

Chyna glanced at Matt. Yes, I want something, she thought. Something that's very bad for me in the long run.

Matt misread her look. "Okay," he said, reaching into the sea of glittering objects in the cart. He fished out a necklace and held it aloft. "You like this?" he asked Chyna.

The silvery chain seemed to sparkle. At the end of the chain swayed a shimmering purple stone. Chyna grinned and nodded her head.

"How much for this?" Matt asked the old woman.

"American?" she asked, cocking her head. The short, frayed kerchief slid back on her iron gray hair. Her hazel eyes glittered more than the stone.

Matt turned toward Chyna. "We've got a con artist on our hands. Yes, American," he said to the vendor.

"Twelve dollars," the old woman declared, putting out an incredibly wrinkled hand. Long nails hooked into her palm. Yup, definitely Snow White material, Chyna thought, looking to see if Matt would pay.

He took fifteen dollars out of his wallet. The woman snatched it, then appeared to look mystified as to how to make change.

"Keep it," Matt said, seeing right through her. The woman's grin spread, her face etched with satisfaction. "Your gift, milady," Matt said, presenting the necklace to Chyna.

She turned back to him. "Put it on, please," she instructed.

The leathery-faced old woman watched, beaming. "Bring good luck," she promised.

"Sure did," Matt commented. "At least to you." He turned Chyna around so he could admire the jewel. It nestled between the valley formed by her rounded breasts. "Lucky jewel," he murmured.

In a crowd of countless people Chyna felt suddenly very alone with him. For a moment she was afraid that he was going to trace the chain's path down to its resting place. But he only did so—though very effectively—with his eyes. She cleared her throat nervously, feeling her own thoughts drifting back to the hotel room. "I thought we were going to take in some sights."

"I am," he told her, looking up. The sparkle had returned to his eyes, teasing her. "I am."

"Different sights," she clarified, taking his arm and pulling him toward the Jeep.

"To each his own," he protested, climbing in behind the wheel. "Okay, where to?" he asked.

For that she had no answer. "I don't know. Someplace terrific."

"We were just there," he told her, looking over her head at the hotel that loomed in the background.

"Don't you have a map?" she asked.

"I like feeling my way around," he answered, his voice low and teasing.

Chyna gritted her teeth. "Of Manila," she pressed.

"In the glove compartment," he offered, still watching her. He liked the way the sunbeams danced through her hair. He longed to reach out and touch the silky strands himself.

"Now we're getting somewhere," Chyna said, reading the summary in one corner of the map citing the tourist attractions.

"I'm glad one of us is," Matt said quite audibly. But

Chyna pretended not to hear. "Let's go here," she said, pointing to a spot on the map.

"Here" was the Ayuntamiento, the seat of the government during the Spanish regime and the early days of the American occupation. Along the border of the square was the Governor's Palace, known as the Palacio Real. It was in ruins, and Matt watched her as she picked her way through the crumbling rubble.

"And here we have the site of a gag that didn't quite come off," he said, using the voice of a tour guide as he followed her up an incline.

"Very funny," she retorted. But she couldn't suppress the smile that formed on her face. In front of them was the most breathtaking sunset she had ever seen. A multitude of colors swirled across the sky as the fading sun dipped down. The final rays washed over the ruins before they were eventually cast into darkness.

"There's nothing funny about the way I'm feeling right now," Matt said, joining her beside a crumbling wall that barely hinted at the beauty that had once existed here.

She knew she shouldn't say anything in answer to his words. She knew she would be better off just going on with her little tour. But a force stronger than her will made her ask, "And what are you feeling?"

Incredibly strong arms went around her, pulling her toward him. "Like if I don't have you soon, I'll take you right here in the ruins."

Steady. Keep your voice steady, she told herself. "It'd probably be the most exciting thing that's happened here in a long time." Did that sound as light as she wanted it to? It was hard to speak coherently when all your pulses were throbbing madly, she thought.

"You're driving me mad, woman," he said, his voice tight with controlled desire.

Each breath he took vibrated against her body as he held her close to him. When he kissed her, everything she had been holding back, everything she had thought was so well repressed, sprang forth like a winged fury. Her limbs were turned to liquid as she clung to him, her arms entwined about his neck, her lips sealed to his.

"You don't want to go on playing the eager tourist," he said softly. It wasn't a question, it was a statement, one she didn't have the energy to quarrel with. It was true. All she wanted was him.

Slowly she shook her head no. The sparkle in his eyes gave way to a look of devastating tenderness, and that was her final undoing. She let him take her hand and lead her back to the Jeep.

She didn't remember the trip back to the hotel. All she was aware of was his presence and the presence of a thousand excited sensations in her body, all waiting for fulfillment.

"Are you hungry?" Matt asked as he opened the door of the hotel room. It had been hours since they had eaten anything.

Yes, she thought, but not for anything that room service can bring me. Aloud she said, "No."

Stop looking at him like that, she ordered. You're going to make him think that his little scheme is working. You're going to make him think that you're even more eager than you probably look.

But she was eager, eager for the feel of his hands on her skin, his lips on hers, for the closeness they could share.

Matt put down the phone, room service and dinner

temporarily forgotten. "Neither am I," he murmured, moving toward her. "The thing I like best," he said, beginning to slowly unbutton the front of her blouse, taking his time with each button, "about being in a hot climate is that there are so few clothes to put on. Or take off." His green eyes bore deep into her soul, holding her captive as she felt each button leave its hole, further parting the material that covered her breasts. The liquid within her limbs was turning into molten lava as she waited for him to finish.

When the blouse finally hung open he eased first one side and then the other off her shoulders. Ever so lightly, he ran his fingers along the swell of her breasts. Chyna was rapidly losing control of her breathing as the blouse fell to the floor. The situation became critical by the time he started working the catch loose on her shorts. He hastened their descent to the thickly carpeted floor with his hands, guiding the light material slowly along her smooth, tanned hips and caressing her thighs with it before he finally let the shorts fall. She stood before him dressed in underwear which displayed more than it covered.

"You look good in pink," he told her huskily, stroking the lacy pink bra, running his finger along the delicately scalloped edges.

He was playing with her, reducing her to mindless passion, and she couldn't do a thing about it.

"But you look even better without it." He whispered the words against the hollow of her throat as she tilted her head back, welcoming his kiss. Behind her, she could feel him releasing the clasp that held her bra together. Within a moment it didn't exist at all, and she felt the imprint of his chest against hers. His hands were on her hips, gently massaging them as he pressed them against his hardened frame. With each pass of his hand her underwear slipped a little lower, teasing the length of her thigh until that last scrap of lace floated away.

The fire grew as the refrain of an old song drifted into her head. "Black magic," she whispered as she curled her fingers along the ridges of his muscular back.

"What?" He raised his head, momentarily refraining from trailing further kisses in a sensuous path toward her breasts.

"That's what you practice," she told him, her voice thick with desire. She saw him through a haze, the light from the lamps in the room seeming to glow like candles.

"A guy's got to do something when he's trying to capture the attention of a fearless stuntwoman." His kisses, small, delicate and overwhelming, were creating havoc as they once again began to descend.

"You have my attention," she gasped, arching her back, inviting him to go on.

"Undivided?" he asked, a tender smile curving his sensuous lips.

"Undivided," she breathed, reveling in the emotions he was awakening within her.

Although he had taken his time undressing her, he wasted none on his own clothes. Before she knew it, he was as devoid of clothing as she was, and then he lifted her into his arms and carried her into the bedroom. The room was cocooned in the somber shades of dusk, but Chyna didn't care. She and Matt made their own light.

As he branded her trembling body with the hot seal of his own, Chyna felt a myriad of sensation exploding within her again. It was as if there were a secret trigger inside her that only he knew how to set off. And he could set it off with just a touch, just by the simple pressure of his body against hers.

The flames grew more intense, licking at her sides, consuming her and making her yearn for him with a force that frightened her. She tried to analyze her feelings, but she couldn't concentrate on anything. All she could do was feel, and the feeling was wonderful.

Lightning flashed through her veins as he molded her to him, pressing her buttocks with the flat of his hand. Vainly she tried to absorb all the heat his body emitted, collecting it inside of her. Unconsciously she was trying to store it against the day when all this would end. Even in her euphoric state, she knew that day would come.

Over and over and over again, Matt's mouth moved over hers, no longer gentle, no longer patient. He wanted her, wanted her as urgently as she wanted him. There were no more games, no more holding back. Paradise could be held at bay only so long.

"I've wanted you all day." Matt rasped against her mouth. "You were driving me out of my mind."

"Was I?" she asked as her breathlessness increased.

"If I couldn't have had you tonight, I would have been certifiably crazy by morning."

She felt his weight shift onto her, saw the smoldering need in his eyes. "I wouldn't want to be the one to shut down production," she whispered, moving to admit him.

"That's my girl," he murmured against her ear.

She had no time to explore the meaning behind his words, no time to wonder if what she was doing was sheer, wanton folly on her part and if she was playing right into his hands. All she knew was utter desire, utter love.

Off-key birds woke her the following morning. She turned her head and realized that her body was curled against Matt's. He was still asleep, a lazy, contented smile on his lips. The rising sun was sprinkling shimmering golden rays through the window, making his hair seem even blonder than it was. He looked like an innocent.

Some innocent, she thought. No innocent could do what he had done to her last night. Last night. The memory of it came back to her, bringing with it a fresh rush of euphoria. It had been wonderful, incredibly wonderful. She sighed and closed her eyes, sinking down into the pillow beneath her head. For a moment she let her feelings roam free, unhampered by cold facts. In the back of her mind she suspected that all this had been orchestrated. But somehow, emotionally, she hoped that perhaps he *did* care just a little, that some of the words he had said to her were true. It would be a start, she thought happily. A start in making him love her. That was all she really wanted.

The birds continued their cacophonous song, nudging her into consciousness. They had to be getting back. She hadn't meant to stay overnight. She had to practice. But then, she hadn't meant for a lot of things to happen, and they had. She shook his shoulder gently, thrilling to the cool, sleek lines of his body as it stirred against her.

"Hey," she said softly, "time to get up, sleepy-head."

One sexy eye opened. "I'm ready," he murmured, reaching for her.

"I didn't mean *that,*" she laughed. "Don't you ever get enough?"

"Not lately," he said. "Not since you've entered my life. I feel like I'm insatiable."

How she wished she could believe him. But she was too much of a realist . . . or was she?

"Hey," Matt said, turning her attention back to him. He tugged the edge of the clinging sheet off her breasts, exposing them totally to his view. "Your neck is green."

"What?" Her hand flew up as she glanced down and caught light green track marks along the upper part of her chest. "It seems your gift has branded me," she said philosophically, digging into the hair at the base of her neck and searching for the clasp.

"Only my gift?" he asked, watching her. Her every movement aroused him.

She wanted to say a lot of things in answer to his question. She wanted to ask a lot of questions of her own. But she couldn't, not yet, so she hid behind a joke. "You don't leave green marks, if that's what you mean," she said, reaching to put the necklace on the nightstand next to her.

"No," he said seriously, pulling her back down and into his arms, "that's not what I mean."

The necklace fell from her fingers as Matt took what was already his.

"I thought you'd be gone longer," were the first words out of Dussault's mouth when Chyna walked past him, heading toward the site of her fight rehearsal. He was annoyed, and the words were seared into Chyna's brain. There, that's for all those castles in the sky you're trying to build, she told herself, searching

for Alex. Taking you to the city was all just part of
Matt's plan to keep your mind off the movie, nothing
more.

Chyna felt a chill even though sun shone as brightly
as ever.

The pace on the set became even more hectic than
usual as the days passed. Dussault was determined to
stay within the original tight schedule. He cajoled,
prodded and screamed in order to get the most out of
his actors. He went directly to screaming, bypassing
the first two, when it came to the extras and the
stuntworkers, Chyna observed. She tried to focus her
attention on her work, but it wasn't easy concentrating. Her thoughts were constantly invaded by memories of the moments she had shared with Matt. He was
infiltrating all her thoughts, both waking and sleeping.
She found herself listening for his step, watching for
his shadow to cross her path. She was, she admitted to
herself, in love. In love with a man who probably just
saw her as part of his job. She should have been
indignant, or at least annoyed. But annoyance was the
last thing on her mind whenever she was near him.

For one thing, it was difficult to be annoyed with a
man who looked forward to his daughter's arrival with
such anticipation. The glow that came into Matt's eyes
when he talked about Meredith convinced Chyna that
he was a warm, loving man. It gave her hope that
everything that had happened between them wasn't
just pretense.

"Meredith, this is Chyna O'Brien," Matt said, intro-
ducing his daughter. "She jumps over burning gasoline tanks for a living."

To Chyna's surprise, the little girl took the statement in stride, extending her hand solemnly to Chyna. She caught herself thinking that Meredith was the most solemn-looking five-year-old she had ever seen. She looked like a model for children's clothes and not a thing like a child who had just finished an exhausting plane ride, topped off with a bumpy trip in a Jeep.

Chyna flashed Meredith her widest smile and had it politely returned. She looked uncertainly over the child's dark head.

Matt beamed. "Great manners," he enthused.

Too great, Chyna thought, still smiling at the child.

And then Chyna saw Wanda, who was standing in the rear of the trailer. Now that she saw her, Chyna couldn't understand how she could have missed the woman, who looked as if she would have been more at home in a Wagnerian opera, wearing a horned helmet and metal breast shield. A very large metal breast shield. She stood like the personification of sternness regarding Chyna.

So this is what an unflappable housekeeper looks like, Chyna thought.

Chyna could see the dark brows narrowing as the woman leveled her gaze at her. "I think I just flunked her appraisal," Chyna whispered, ducking her head so that Wanda wouldn't be able to read her lips.

"That's okay," Matt said, putting his arm around her shoulders. "As long as you pass mine."

"Well, Meredith, why don't you change into something more comfortable and I'll show you around," Chyna volunteered. The vanguard in the rear moved in closer. "You too, Wanda," Chyna added, forcing an inviting smile.

The face that looked back at her was stony. "I've seen enough sound stages to last me a lifetime," Wanda told her, turning her down.

"I take it that means no," Chyna said, turning questioningly toward Matt.

"Wanda used to be in movies," Matt explained.

Monster Madness in Manhattan, no doubt, Chyna thought. "Well, then, we won't bore you," she declared, then looked down at Meredith. "How about you?"

"Yes, please. If daddy can come, too."

"Daddy is most certainly welcome," Chyna said spiritedly. "It's his picture."

In response Matt grinned and nodded. They shared a tiny moment in private, despite Wanda's presence. She needed that, Chyna thought, heartened. How quickly she had become dependent on his smile. Addicting stuff, she told herself. So was his lovemaking. The more she got, the more she wanted. Enough, her wavering discipline pleaded.

"Don't you want to change?" Chyna asked Meredith, trying to pull herself out of the deep cauldron of emotion she felt herself falling into.

But Meredith shook her head. "I'll be fine, thank you."

"Isn't she terrific?" Matt asked, ushering them both out the door.

"Terrific," Chyna agreed. And restrained, she added silently. The children she encountered were never this reserved. And even when they appeared to be as polite as Meredith, there was always a hint of mischief in their eyes. No such hint existed here. She wondered what had happened to make the little girl that way.

But for the time being Chyna kept her questions to herself as she followed Matt and Meredith out the door.

"Damn it, man, if you were any more wooden, you'd be a prime candidate for Dutch Elm Disease!" Dussault spat, yelling at the leading man as Chyna and the others approached the shooting site.

"I see he took his happy pills this morning," Chyna commented to Matt.

Meredith looked up at Chyna. "They're not working," she observed quietly.

"You bet they're not," Chyna agreed, trying not to laugh out loud.

Dussault heard her voice—though apparently not her words—and whirled to face her, obvious disgust in his eyes. For a moment he didn't see Matt and Meredith. "I thought you were told not to hover around the set unless you were on call," he said nastily.

Chyna cast a glance toward Matt. He had never come out and told her not to "hover." No doubt he felt that actions spoke louder than words. And in her case, they had. But confronted with Dussault's haughtily condescending voice, Chyna was tempted to say something biting in return. She bit her tongue.

"She's not hovering, she's with us," Matt said, his voice sterner than she had ever heard it. She could tell he was annoyed with the way Dussault had spoken to her, and it made her feel warm and protected. She grinned at the silly notion, but hugged it to herself nonetheless.

She saw Dussault's expression change entirely. It became obsequious, although Chyna could have sworn that she detected an underlying layer of resentment, as well.

"Are we going on with this scene or not?" Beaumont called out impatiently. The actor stood with his doubled-up fists on his hips.

Dussault raised his palms upward in exasperated supplication. "The man's so bad, he doesn't even know when we've stopped working." His gaze shifted to Meredith. "And who's this little darling?" he asked, squatting down to Meredith's level.

"My daughter," Matt said needlessly. Chyna wondered if the director would have looked so fawning if Meredith had been her daughter instead of Matt's, then wondered why she'd bothered. She knew the answer to that one.

Her mind skidded to a halt. Her daughter? She slowly turned the unexpected thought over in her head. She looked at the little girl, her dark, delicate features so different from Matt's. She was the image of her mother, no doubt. Except for the eyes. The eyes were green and shadowed with lashes that looked almost too long for her small face. Matt's eyes. Matt's lashes. Yes, she could have a daughter about this age. Except that hers would have smiled more. A lot more.

As they went on Meredith appeared to be content just to march along beside them, her hands at her sides, a miniature adult, but Chyna reached out and grasped her small hand anyway. It was a warm gesture and one that Meredith looked a little uncertain about accepting. Chyna pretended not to notice. She led the "tour" toward where she did her ritual morning exercises.

"What's that?" Meredith asked, pointing.

"That's a trampoline," Chyna said, dropping on one knee to be on eye level with the girl. "It's kind of like a big bed that you jump on—without the pillows. Want to try it?" she offered.

As far as Chyna knew, most kids would have run right over her in their haste to get on. But Meredith just stood there. "I don't jump on beds," she said quietly.

"Wait here," Chyna said, getting back up. She took Matt's hand and drew him aside. "Matt," she said kindly, "what's wrong with her?"

She saw him stiffen slightly. "What do you mean?"

Chyna spread her hands helplessly. "She's so reserved, so polite—it's like someone programmed all the fun out of her. It's not natural."

Matt closed his eyes and sighed. "Laura didn't like children very much, and she didn't keep it a secret from Meredith. Meredith tried to do everything to please her. When she left, Meredith thought it was her fault." He looked over to where his daughter was standing. Chyna could see the torment in his eyes. "She still does," he added quietly.

Chyna found herself profoundly disliking a woman she had never met. Without a word to Matt, she walked back to the little girl.

She lowered her voice as if she were talking to a fellow conspirator. "You're supposed to bounce on it. C'mon, we'll do it together," she urged.

The girl's green eyes opened wide as Chyna took her hand. "Really?" Meredith cried in surprise.

"Really," Chyna told her, lifting the girl up first, then climbing on herself. "Here. I'll hold your hands until you get the hang of this."

Meredith gave her an uncertain, grateful smile,

placing both her hands in Chyna's. Matt just stood back and watched, marveling at Meredith's reaction to Chyna. Usually the girl hung back, intensely shy.

But Meredith was responding to Chyna just the way he had found himself responding to her at first. Warily, uncertainly, yet drawn in by her intensity and warmth. Chyna had more zest for life than anyone he had ever met. He hoped some of that zest could be transferred to Meredith.

"What did you do?" Wanda demanded when they walked back into the trailer. She cast a horrified eye at Meredith, whose formerly neatly-braided hair was now sticking out all over, while her bangs were plastered against her forehead, held in place by a large dose of perspiration. Her dress was rumpled and wilted.

"Had fun," Chyna said proudly, releasing Meredith's hand as she surrendered the girl to Wanda. "Don't worry," she said cheerfully, "she's washable. We do a lot of sweating around here."

Wanda sniffed, but not quite as indignantly as she might have. Firmly taking Meredith by the hand, she marched the girl to the shower.

Matt took Chyna into his arms. "You're incredible, you know that?"

"Yes," she answered brightly, her eyes dancing. "I've been told so. It just took you a little longer than most people to find out, that's all. I'm making allowances for the heat."

"Which heat?" he asked, tracing the outline of her lips. "Yours, or mine?"

"Nature's," she answered.

He kissed the tip of her nose, then worked his way

down to her mouth. "Do you know what I want right now?"

"I think I have a strong suspicion," Chyna laughed, pushing him back slightly. "But you're going to have to be on your best behavior," she reminded him playfully, nodding in the direction Meredith had just taken.

"There's your cabin," he pointed out, tightening his hold around her waist.

"Shack," she corrected. "And Pepper's there."

"I'll fire her," he offered, kissing the point of her shoulder.

"You can't do that," Chyna protested teasingly. "Besides, I've heard that absence makes the heart grow fonder," she said, purposely running her finger along his chest and tracing a pattern around his heart.

"Maybe," he conceded. "But it's hell on the body."

"Daddy!" Meredith called from the bathroom.

"Wanda's probably scrubbing her skin off," Chyna guessed, taking the opportunity to step away from him. "Better go and rescue your daughter. I've got to practice anyway."

"The sky stunt," he remembered.

Chyna nodded, then saw that he looked concerned. Was that for show? Or was some of it real? "There's a plane involved," she assured him. "I don't just pop out of space."

"How do you practice something like that?" he asked.

"Very, very carefully," she teased, then became more somber. "You don't. Not from that height, anyway. You practice taking smaller jumps. You practice timing. You also practice praying a little," she added with a wink, leaving.

Was he really concerned about her? Had she gotten to him one-tenth as much as he had gotten to her? Had he fallen into his own trap? No, men like Matt didn't fall into traps. She was sure that his bad experience with Laura had colored the way he regarded women in general. And, after all, she had originally taken him to court. Not exactly the best foundation for a romance . . . or something more lasting.

It was up to her to change that, she thought as she headed back to her trampoline.

Work, concentrate on work, she ordered herself. Or else you're not going to be able to concentrate on anything. She found, to her relief, that she could still filter out all extraneous thoughts just before she undertook a gag. Doggedly she worked out her stunt, getting everything down to a science. Fear was the necessary ingredient that compelled her to triple-check everything before she started. But once that checking was done, fear was driven out. It had no place in the execution of her stunts. It could only cause her to freeze, something that could be fatal.

Chyna had set her equipment up near a hill that suited her specifications. After making sure that her knee, shin and elbow pads were fastened securely, she paused on the crest. From her vantage point she could see and hear the scene being filmed below her.

"Faster, damn it! Faster! Go faster!" Dussault roared, riding alongside the insert car. In answer to his orders, the driver accelerated even more.

That man was going to kill someone yet, Chyna thought angrily. She waited until the area was clear before she attempted her stunt, sailing down into the waiting air mattress. As she tumbled out of its recesses she saw that filming had come to a halt, and that two of the cameramen were walking by, grumbling audibly.

"You need a drink, kid," the older cameraman was telling his companion, who looked shaken.

"I need a safer profession," the other man answered. There was no missing the tremor in his voice. He ran his hand through a wayward mop of hair. "When we took that curve I damn near fell off."

"But you didn't," the other man said. "That's all that matters."

But it wasn't all that mattered, Chyna thought as she watched the two men walk away. It wasn't all that mattered at all.

10

~-œœœœœœœœœœ-

Chyna thought of going straight to Matt to tell him what she had overheard, then changed her mind. Maybe she was overreacting to the situation. After all, by definition the stunts *had* to be dangerous. Maybe the cameraman she had heard complaining was just exaggerating.

Hold it. What was happening here? She was fabricating excuses for what she knew was going on. Was this the result of Matt's lovemaking? Was he succeeding in his attempt to "handle" the problem her presence generated? She pressed her lips together. A jumble of confused emotions warred within her, pulling her in two different directions. For the time being, she decided to hold her peace and go on practicing.

The sky above her turned an angry purple, then faded into an ominous gray. The sun had completely vanished. Rain, Chyna thought, deciding to cut her practice session short. Out here, she knew, it didn't just rain, it monsooned. Chyna gathered her equipment together. Overhead the wind's low moan grew into a bellow as it raked through the fronds of the palm trees. She passed the beach on her way to her shack and stopped for a moment, fascinated by the sight of the angry surf pounding white, foamy fists against the submissive beach.

It looked like it was going to be a big one, she thought.

Her mind shifted to Dussault. He was going to be furious if he had to stop shooting because of rain. The picture of a raging, frustrated Dussault brought a wide grin to her face. "Yes, Virginia, there is a Santa Claus," she murmured to herself as she began to run back to her quarters, trying to outrace the large drops of rain that had just begun to fall.

She had just made it inside when the large drops joined together to form pelting sheets of rain. Pepper barreled in right behind her, nearly knocking her over. Chyna jumped aside just in time.

"It's only rain, Pepper," Chyna said, laughing. "You won't melt."

"One way or another I keep getting wet out here. If it isn't perspiration because of the heat, it's rain," Pepper muttered, annoyed. Her dutchboy hairdo was plastered to both sides of her face. In a vain attempt to dry off she shook herself, mimicking the motions of a wet dog. Looking at Chyna as she hunted for a towel, she suddenly remembered something and said, "Oh, Mr. Harrigan's looking for you."

"Terrific," Chyna muttered. "He couldn't look for me before the rain started, right? Oh, well, when my master calls . . ." she said loftily, looking around for something to shield her from the rain. The last thing in the world she had thought to pack was an umbrella. After all, who took an umbrella to a tropical paradise? Or a safety net to a love affair? her inner voice whispered. She should have done both—and hadn't.

"Is he?" Pepper asked. She stopped peeling off her wet shorts and looked quizzically at Chyna.

"Is he what?" Chyna asked absently, rummaging through her suitcase. There wasn't anything there that would do the slightest bit of good against the rain for more than fifteen seconds, she thought, letting the lid of the case drop back down.

"Your master."

Chyna caught the inflection in Pepper's voice. The funny, crooked smile on the other woman's guileless face matched it. "He's the producer, remember?" Chyna said evasively. "That makes him *our* master."

"And that's all?" Pepper asked, cocking her head. It was plain she didn't believe any of Chyna's protests.

Chyna didn't bother protesting any further. "Yes," she said firmly. "That's all."

With that she rushed out, bracing herself against the pummeling drops.

Pepper's high voice followed her. "I don't believe you," she singsonged.

"Neither do I," Chyna muttered under her breath as she ran. The palm trees shielded her for part of the way. The rest of the run was out in the open.

"This had better be good," Chyna announced when Matt opened the door, letting her in. Rivulets of rain ran down her face, and she pushed her water-logged hair out of her eyes, wondering if she would ever feel dry again.

"My God," Matt cried, "you're all wet."

"Now I know why you're the producer. You have

the gift of insight," she muttered, squeezing out the hem of her shirt. A puddle formed around her feet. "I look like a wet chicken."

"The most delectable wet chicken I've ever seen," Matt assured her, going in to another room for a moment. He popped back in with a huge, fluffy towel.

She took it from him. "How many wet chickens do you usually see in a week?" she asked as she rubbed the towel along her arms.

"You're the first," he said with a grin. "Why did you come out in this?"

She looked at him, stunned. "Weren't you looking for me?" If he wasn't, she was going to kill Pepper when she got back. When she swam back, she amended, listening to the rain. The metal trailer amplified the sound, making it seem as if the rain were attacking from all directions. Chyna wondered if the trailer could withstand the assault.

"Yes, but I could have waited. There was no need to try to drown yourself . . . or is that some inner compulsion you stuntpeople have?" he teased, watching the way the towel was gliding along her skin. Her blouse and shorts were plastered against her body, outlining every single detail. He felt an urge to follow the path blazed by the towel, but he held himself in check.

"No," she retorted, "but we're polite. When we're told someone is looking for us, we usually turn up." She began drying her hair, rubbing vigorously. She wound up with a tousled, wavy look. "Well, I'm here, so what's on your mind?" she asked, running her fingers through her dripping hair, wishing she looked better.

"Lots," he murmured. The warm glow in his eyes

pleased her. Maybe he liked wet women. "But I have to be on my best behavior," he said with a sigh.

"Ah, a first, no doubt," she laughed.

Wanda bustled in just then. There was no other word to describe the woman's entrance, Chyna thought. Wanda "bustled" everywhere she went, her huge hips swaying. "I've finally calmed her down," she announced to Matt.

"Meredith's afraid of storms?" Chyna guessed, looking up at Matt.

He nodded. "It's a new phase."

She thought of her own childhood and the time when she had been frightened of the loud noises that came rumbling out of the angry skies. She had always had a warm haven to retreat to. Her father always seemed to be there when she needed him, especially after her mother had died. Chyna's heart went out to the little girl in the next room as she thought of the times when Matt had been away and the only person Meredith had been able to seek comfort from was Wanda-with-the-iron-expression. The woman might be fond of the child, Chyna thought, but she was light years away from being warm and toasty.

"Is she asleep?" Chyna asked Wanda.

"No, but—"

"Excuse me," Chyna said, pushing past her. It was, she thought drolly, one of her more difficult stunts, given the narrow width of the passageway.

When she entered the room Chyna found Meredith in bed, her huddled body outlined beneath the blanket. She looked as if she were trying to pull herself into the smallest ball she could. Very quietly Chyna sat down on the bed. Meredith stuck her head out and looked at her.

"Oh," she cried, surprised. Her expression was uncertain, yet pleased. She looked, Chyna thought, relieved. Chyna had been right. She needed company.

"I've been out," Chyna explained, realizing that her appearance was a little startling. "Walking in the rain."

Meredith sat up. The pale face became animated, a conspiratorial glow entering it. "Weren't you afraid?" she asked, her voice hushed.

"There's nothing to be afraid of, except maybe catching a cold," Chyna told her, glancing at Matt, who was standing quietly in the doorway.

Meredith turned her face toward the window and watched the rain lash at the pane. The world beyond the room looked dark and foreboding. Another loud crash of thunder rocked the room. Meredith dove for the haven of Chyna's arms. "It sounds so scary."

Chyna pulled her closer. "When you get bigger you'll find that a lot of loud noises are only that—loud noises. If you stand up to them you'll see that there's nothing to be afraid of at all," she assured her, giving the girl a warm squeeze.

Meredith looked up into her face. "Were you ever afraid of storms?" she asked.

Chyna laughed. "Scared stiff," she confided. "I used to run into my daddy's study and crawl under his desk. And you know what he'd do?"

Meredith shook her head, solemnly waiting for the answer.

"He'd pick me up and hold me on his lap and tell me stories until the storm was over—or until I felt brave enough not to be afraid." Chyna smiled at the trusting, upturned face. "Want me to tell you a story?"

The vigorous nod was all she needed.

She had nearly exhausted her entire repertoire of stories before Meredith finally drifted off to sleep. Gently Chyna eased her down and Matt tucked her in. He put his arm around Chyna's shoulders and they walked out.

"I'm not sure who enjoyed those stories more, you or Meredith," Chyna teased, her voice cracking a little. "I never thought I'd say this after my trek over here, but could I have a glass of water? My throat feels like the Mohave Desert."

"Anything for the master storyteller," he said lightly, going over to the sink. He handed a filled glass to her, his eyes smiling. "You're really something else, Chyna O'Brien."

She practically gulped down the entire glass in one swallow, then sighed, handing it back to him. "I thought you already knew that," she said wryly.

He put the glass down on the tiny kitchen counter behind him. "I've just taken a refresher course." There was a cough from the couch. They both looked in that direction. "She's asleep, Wanda. I won't be needing you anymore tonight."

Wanda rose. "If you want to be alone," she said in her no-nonsense voice, "just say so."

"I want to be alone, Wanda," Matt said, a degree of amusement and affection in his voice.

"She's really an ex-actress?" Chyna asked, looking over her shoulder as the full-figured woman disappeared into Meredith's room, where an extra cot had been set up.

"Absolutely," Matt confirmed, ushering Chyna over to the couch.

"Hmm, remind me to catch some of the old horror

movies on the late show," Chyna muttered, sitting down.

"Wanda's all right," Matt assured her.

Chyna shrugged. "If you say so. Personally, I'd check her for fangs."

"And what should I check you for?" he asked, moving in closer. His thigh pressed against hers, stirring a response within her before she even realized it was happening.

"Sanity, for one," she quipped.

"Why?" he asked, his eyes glowing with some unidentifiable emotion. "Because you're beginning to feel something for me?"

She would have liked to have put him in his place for being so terribly sure of himself. Unfortunately, most of her wanted him to stay right where he was. She was feeling something for him, all right. More than just a small something, and it was clouding her vision. Recalling the conversation she had overheard between him and Dussault didn't remedy the situation at all. She was in love with him.

"No," she answered crisply. "Because I came out in this monsoon when Pepper said you were looking for me. What *was* it you wanted, anyway?"

"To ask you to Meredith's birthday party. I just mentioned it in passing to Pepper before the down-pour started. I didn't mean for you to risk life and limb," he said, allowing his hand to roam leisurely along her thigh.

"Didn't you?" she asked meaningfully, struggling hard not to sway in her seat. Throbbing anticipation which she knew could not be fulfilled that night sprang up wherever his hand passed.

"Do all stuntpeople talk in riddles?" he asked, brushing aside her hair and kissing the sensitive area of her neck.

"It's one of our small pleasures," she murmured, momentarily losing some of the control she was trying so valiantly to exercise. He could create ecstasy for her so quickly.

"Name another small pleasure," he coaxed, following the line of her collar with light, tingling kisses. Desire began to bloom.

"It's not so small," she admitted, but refused to give it a name. "Not by a long shot. But you have to be good," she reminded him, pressing her hands against his chest. She had pushed harder in her lifetime, she thought.

But her action stopped him. "Parenthood," he decided, sighing heavily, "is not without its trials."

Chyna took two deep breaths before she went on, her voice still sounding a little shaky. "So," she said, trying to sound breezy, "what have you got planned for her birthday?" she asked.

Her question threw him. "Planned?" he asked, confused. "A cake. Candles. You know, the usual."

"I thought you big Hollywood types threw outlandish parties for your kids, complete with rented circuses and things." She shook her head. "You're getting to be a big disappointment to me, Harrigan." Her eyes twinkled as she spoke.

"Am I, now?" The look he gave her warmed her to the very core. But then he laughed. "Maybe you haven't noticed this little fact," he went on, his hand still resting on her thigh, still stirring her, "but we're not exactly in L.A. at the moment."

"So that's why I haven't found the freeway!" she

quipped, enjoying their lighthearted exchange, enjoying sharing a smile with him.

"Drink?" he offered, gesturing toward the compact bar in the corner.

"A screwdriver," she said slowly as an idea began forming. "Just because you've got a lousy work schedule," she said, getting up and walking over to him, "doesn't mean that you have to deprive her." Leaning her elbows on the counter, she watched as he poured orange juice into a glass, following it with a shot of vodka.

He handed her the glass, but rather than drink, she put it down on the counter. It immediately formed a ring around its base. She moved it around as she talked, making intersecting circles.

"Okay, just what is it you have in mind for my poor, deprived daughter?" Matt asked, eyeing her. "Or shouldn't I ask?"

"Sure you should ask," Chyna said. "How else are you going to find out?" Before he had a chance to comment about her talking in riddles again, she went on, her voice growing in momentum as she spoke. "You might not have a circus here, but you do have stuntpeople."

"How well I know that," Matt said, taking a long drink from his glass. The ice cubes clinked back down as he set his glass next to hers.

"None of your sarcasm, Harrigan," Chyna warned, "or I won't tell you my wonderful plan."

He wrapped his arms around her waist, pulling her against him, and breathed in the sweet scent that was hers alone. The rain hadn't washed it away. "Just so long as you don't go away," he murmured. "Okay, and just what is this wonderful plan?"

"We can dress up as clowns and do tricks for her. Nothing overwhelming, just a few simple things. Something that would make a five-year-old's eyes grow wide," she told him, letting her own arms surround him. She liked the warmth he ignited within her. She just hoped it wasn't an illusion created by his own brand of special effects.

"Wanna make a thirty-two-year-old's eyes grow wide?" he asked, nibbling on her ear.

The sultry feeling of his breath against her cheek began to resurrect that by now familiar liquid sensation within her. "What is this, a test?" she asked. "Are you trying to see how long I can keep my hands off you?" She snuggled in closer. "If it is, you don't fight very fair."

"I never claimed to be a fair fighter," he reminded her. "Just a good one."

No, he had never claimed to fight fair, she agreed. And she was the casualty. "Well, I guess it's up to me to enforce the rules regarding your good behavior." She disengaged herself from his arms. "I've got to be going," she told him, backing away.

"But it's still raining," Matt said, pointing toward the window. "You'll get wet."

And if I stay here, I'll get burned, she thought. "That's okay." She shrugged. "I'm a wash and wear model," she cracked as she opened the door.

He caught her arm as she began to go outside. "And I'd like to wear it," he told her, holding her against him. The door flew completely open, pushed flat against the side of the trailer by the force of the wind. Sheets of rain began to come inside, but Matt didn't seem to notice as he kissed her fiercely. She felt the raw emotion that was churning within him rise to the surface.

It was all she could do to draw her lips from his and wedge her hands between them. "Not today," she breathed. "I'm not making love to a man who doesn't have enough sense to come in out of the rain."

And with that she fled into the downpour, though she turned back once to wave at him. He was still standing in the open doorway, the rain lashing at him. "What a mess," she muttered as she ran.

The rain stung her face, momentarily taking her mind off the dilemma she was in. Although Matt's feelings for her seemed genuine, Chyna couldn't rid herself of the fears created by the words she had heard him say to Dussault.

All right, even if it wasn't all an act, so what? People got close when they worked together. Once the movie was over, so was the romance. Matt was a busy producer. A lot of glamorous, willing women came his way. Why would he want to continue a liaison with a woman whom his peers viewed as a trouble-maker?

You think too much, she told herself as she reached the door of her shack.

The storm lasted into the next day, throwing the entire shooting schedule further behind than it already was. Because of their location, there was precious little for the cast and crew to do. For most, boredom set in long before noon. Felicia, the wardrobe mistress, however, found that she had no such problem.

"Clown costumes?" she asked, staring at Chyna, who had just told her about the project for Meredith's birthday. "He wants five clown costumes by tomorrow?" she cried.

"He" was Matt. Chyna had known that she wouldn't get very far with the older woman if she said she was the one who wanted the costumes.

The plump wardrobe mistress stood surrounded by a variety of fabrics, buttons and other ingredients that could magically be converted into costumes at the right moment—after a great deal of muttering and snipping. Felicia spread her hands helplessly. "And just how does he expect me to do that?" she demanded.

Chyna shook her head in sympathy. Pepper, witnessing the charade, choked back a laugh. "You know how these producers are," Chyna said, "always demanding the impossible. But if anyone can do it, Felicia, you can."

"But I don't even know any sizes. I—" The wail turned into unintelligible sputterings as Felicia sifted through a large multi-colored heap of material.

"Medium," Chyna said. "Medium's safe," she assured the woman, despite Pepper's nudge to her own ribs. "If the costumes don't fit, so much the better. Who ever heard of a well-dressed clown, anyway?"

"It can't be done," the woman informed Chyna as both she and Pepper edged out of the room. But it was.

Chyna also managed to convince three other stunt-workers to join her and Pepper in acting out the half-formed scenerio she had come up with.

"There's not going to be enough room to perform in the trailer," Scottie, one of the stuntmen, pointed out. "I don't sky dive too well from the top of a refrigerator."

Chyna remained undaunted. "The weather will clear up," she promised. And if it didn't, she'd come up with something else, she added silently.

"Do I have to put this on?" Pepper wailed the next day as she looked beseechingly at Chyna. Chyna sat on her cot, juggling a mirror she had purloined from the prop department and some foundation and blusher that she had gotten as a grudging gift from the makeup department. She glanced at the pot of white face-paint that Pepper was holding.

"You can't be a clown without makeup," Chyna told her, drawing in a broad mouth on her own white face.

"I'll start a new trend," Pepper said hopefully.

Chyna thrust the paint toward her friend. "It washes off," she promised.

Pepper frowned deeply as she sat down, following Chyna's lead. Outside, the sun was beginning to shine.

"Is there anything you can't do?" Matt asked Chyna later after she and the other clowns came tumbling out of Chyna and Pepper's shack, much to the glee of Meredith.

"Off hand," Chyna said, stepping out of the way as two clowns in blue went into their hastily conceived act, "I can think of one or two things."

"Such as?" Matt asked, his eyes on Meredith's beaming face.

Such as convincing myself that all this is real, Chyna thought sadly. "This is no time to get serious," she told him.

He caught her hand as she moved to join the others. "Remind me to get serious soon," he whispered.

She knew he didn't mean what she did, but she smiled beneath the painted-on red mouth. "I'll remind you."

"It's the very best party I've ever, ever had!" Meredith cried, wrapping her arms around Chyna's black-and-white checkered waist.

It was Chyna's turn to beam with pleasure. The animated little girl before her was light years away from the subdued short adult she had met in Matt's trailer.

"Glad you liked it," Chyna said affectionately, ruffling the girl's hair. "Thanks, everybody," she called to the other clowns as they began to leave.

Murmurs of "Don't mention it," and "Happy birthday, Meredith," filled the air as they left. Matt came over to Chyna as Wanda began gathering up the litter left over from the party.

"Here," he said, offering the box of tissues he was carrying. "It's time for the fairy godmother to reappear."

"Is that what I am?" Chyna asked with a laugh.

He took a tissue out of the box and began to wipe away the red paint around her mouth. "You are to her," he said, nodding at Meredith.

The happy smile on the little girl's face confirmed Matt's words. "I need cold cream to get this off," Chyna told Matt, taking the smeared tissue away from him.

"Were you scared, Chyna?" Meredith asked.

The question came totally out of the blue. "When?" Chyna thought that the stunts she had done at the party were pretty tame.

"Daddy said you jumped over an exploding gas

tank. He showed me the movie. Were you scared?" she asked again.

Chyna turned to look at Matt. "You have the rushes?" she asked. Normally the rushes were sent back to the parent studio the next day, and she had done the stunt a couple of weeks ago.

"I have a copy."

How odd, she thought. Then she realized that she hadn't answered Meredith's question. "No," she said, taking the girl by the hand and beginning to walk back to the trailer. "I wasn't afraid. There are a lot more frightening things in life than the stunts I do."

"What are they?" Meredith asked, unable to imagine anything more frightening than jumping over exploding tanks.

"Someday when you're older I'll tell you," Chyna said, turning for a moment to look back at Matt.

He was busy picking up Meredith's gifts and missed the solemn expression on her face.

11

oooooooooo

Work resumed at a fever pitch. Two days of filming had been lost, and Dussault was absolutely determined to make them up. He drove everyone relentlessly . . . not to mention crazy, Chyna thought, watching him from the sidelines as he readied everyone for the huge fight scene. Normally something involving so many stuntworkers would have taken nearly a week to rehearse and film. Each piece of the fight had to be separately choreographed, and camera angles had to be just so in order to fool the audience. More injuries were sustained during fight scenes than in any other stunt. Putting the sequences together to minimize risks took time and patience. Dussault had neither.

He was just as determined to get the fire sequence under wraps. Like the fight scene, it required the combined talents of all fifteen stuntworkers. Dussault ordered rehearsals for both scenes to be carried on back to back.

"Why not simultaneously?" Chyna muttered to Matt that night in his trailer. "That way we can swing and fight fire, swing and fight fire." She pressed her lips together in exasperation. "Matt . . ."

Matt raised his hands in defense. "Yes, yes, I know. He's getting a little out of hand."

"A little?" she cried. Was his phrasing just poor, or was he really blind to what was going on?

"The man is only trying to do his job," Matt pointed out. "Believe me, I know Phil. He's really not as bad as you seem to think he is. During filming he becomes a little obsessed at times, but there have never been any major accidents on his sets."

Chyna wondered just what Matt thought was a major accident, but she let him go on talking.

"And there won't be any on this picture, either," he told her when he saw the look of doubt in her eyes. He took her hands in his. "But if it'll make you feel any better, I'll talk to him."

"Promise?" she asked, eyeing him dubiously. Was this to put her off her guard? Or did he really mean it?

"I promise."

Matt sat down on the couch, pulling her onto his lap as he did so. It was clear that right then he had other things on his mind, but Chyna wouldn't let the matter drop. Still, she decided to put in the last words on the subject playfully.

"Remember," she warned, wagging her finger in front of him, "if you break your promise, I won't give you any peace."

"Is that a promise or a threat?" he teased.

"Take it any way you like."

He nipped her ear. Instantly Chyna was propelled into another world, a world populated only by the two of them. "I'll take it any way I can," he said just before he kissed her.

"Does that mean you like my daddy?"

The kiss ended abruptly. Chyna found it hard to kiss Matt when she was laughing. "Yes," she answered unabashedly, standing up, "I like your daddy."

Meredith had walked into the trailer, followed by her formidable escort. The child's next question was a little harder to handle. "Will you be going home with us?" she asked, her wide eyes hopeful.

Chyna ran her hand over the dark head, smiling fondly at the girl. "Nope. I have a film to make. And your daddy won't be coming home for a little while, either, I'm afraid. He's going to stay until we're all finished here."

For a moment the little face fell. But then Meredith considered the matter. "Will you take care of him?" she asked Chyna.

Chyna bit her lip, trying hard not to laugh again. She raised her right hand solemnly. "I'll take care of him."

"Okay," Meredith agreed. "I'll go home with Wanda." A yawn escaped her as she spoke.

"Time for bed," Matt instructed. "You've got a big day ahead of you tomorrow." Obediently Meredith went off to bed, with Wanda more than amply bringing up the rear. "I'll be there to tuck you in in a few minutes," Matt called after them.

"How about you?" he asked, turning back to Chyna and fingering the white lace tie on the front of her shirt. "Can I tuck you in, too?" he asked. The

words were soft, sultry. Chyna could feel the familiar
stirrings beginning.

But she shook her head. "I've got a big day
tomorrow, too. Besides," she reminded him, her eyes
shining mischievously, "there's no place for us to go."

"There's my room," he whispered into her hair as
he drew her close to him. "You remember my bed,
don't you? The site of our first meeting of the minds,
so to speak." His words were teasing, but they were
brimming with barely concealed desire.

"Meredith's in the next room," she protested,
weakening despite her self. How long since she had
last loved him? Too long.

"She's given us her blessing," Matt said, beginning
to part the lacing down the front of her shirt. Flames
ignited everywhere he touched her. The ache she felt
grew nearly unbearable.

"She might have," Chyna agreed, "but Wanda is
still in there with her. And I've no doubt that she's got
ears like a bat." She felt herself melting against him.
The separation had been too long, her body cried. Not
long enough, her mind insisted. She was still unable to
think straight around him.

Her internal war was forgotten as his kiss brushed
against her lips.

"I promise to be very, very quiet. Wanda won't
even know I've gone to bed. Only you'll know." It was
a sensuous promise that did wild things to her pulse.
So did the tiny kisses he was sprinkling liberally about
her mouth.

Chyna let herself be led off without offering another
word of protest. She was in no shape to protest
anything, she thought as she followed him, her hand
securely in his.

Her hand was the only thing that *was* secure, a little voice reminded her. Even though she appeared to fit so well into the little family scene that had been unfolding over the last few days, she was still plagued by doubts. Would she be a part of Matt's life once this movie was over? But her doubts weren't strong enough to keep her from loving him, from wanting him with every shred of her being.

Matt opened the door to his room and ushered her in. "There's something to be said for small places," he whispered softly against the nape of her neck, snuggling against her and teasing her with his body.

"Yes," Chyna whispered back, "they're maddening. Don't forget, you promised to tuck Meredith in," she reminded him.

His expression told her that he *had* forgotten. "You make me forget a lot of things," he told Chyna affectionately. "Wait right here."

And wait she did, although her common sense, slowly returning in the wake of his absence, told her to go. The more dependent she became on his lovemaking, the harder it would be for her later, but she couldn't help herself. She stayed, anxiously anticipating the glory of his touch.

She didn't have long to wait.

"Sorry," he murmured, kissing her temple. "Where were we?"

She reached up and took his face in her hands, moving his lips to hers. "Here."

He seemed to delight in arousing her. Her response grew with each caress, each kiss that touched a different part of her anatomy. He lingered over every part, branding it with kisses that alternated between soft and tender, and passionately urgent.

The undulations of her hips grew demanding as his tongue tickled her navel, circling it with kisses that were only half playful. Most exciting of all was the fact that his own breathing was increasing. She adored exciting him. But at this point she was beyond being able to do anything on her own. She was nearly numb with ecstasy.

"Matt . . ." She half whispered, half moaned his name, wanting him to come back up to her level, wanting to savor the taste of his mouth on hers.

"Shh," he chided. "Don't disturb the producer at work. This is a delicate project." His words warmed the sensitive skin of her inner thigh, his breath caressing it before his mouth did.

"Your . . . project . . . is turning into an . . . epic," she complained breathlessly.

"I don't believe in filming shorts," he said, pausing for a second before his tongue took intimate possession of her.

Chyna bit her lip hard to keep from moaning audibly. Her fingers buried themselves in his thick, blond hair. "Please," she pleaded. "Come to me." *Before I scream out loud,* she added silently, not knowing how much longer she could endure what was happening to her.

And then he was above her, a tender look in his eyes. A man like this had to be able to love, she thought. He just *had* to.

It was the last thought she was capable of as ecstasy pushed everything else out of her mind. As he took her, she joined him in the intimate duet that was theirs alone.

She pulled his mouth over hers to keep from crying out. And when it was over Chyna sighed, falling back against the pillow. Trying to steady her erratic pulse, she took a deep breath, hoping the air would clear her head. All she could smell was a mixture of cologne and body scent that was his alone. She smiled deeply, a feeling of incredible contentment spreading through her.

"You do good work," she whispered. "This was by far the greatest epic I've ever been in." She meant to sound light and teasing, but she didn't have enough strength to do anything except whisper the words.

Matt kissed her cheek tenderly, lying down next to her and cradling her in his arms. "When properly inspired, I can be a genius," he said. "And you're the greatest inspiration of my life."

Was she? Was she really? There were a million questions she wanted to ask him, but she was too tired. All she could do was hang on to the feeling his words had awoken within her. Some men did lie at times like this, she thought, trying to temper the joy she felt, but it refused to be dampened.

Reaching out, she ran her finger along his lips. He held her hand and kissed each finger lightly.

"I want to thank you," he said.

"For what?" she asked, puzzled.

"For the way you've been with Meredith. She's changed so much." He looked down into her face. "And it's all because of you."

Chyna shrugged his words away. "A person would have to be made out of stone not to respond to her."

Matt looked away for a moment, staring past her shoulder. "I was led to believe that gung-ho career women were too self-centered to care about other people."

She ached for him. He looked so vulnerable at that

moment. Gently she touched his face, and he brought his gaze back to her. "Did she hurt you very much?" she whispered.

"Who?"

"Laura." She had no place prying this way, but feeling the way she did about Matt, she couldn't help herself.

"I survived," he said, closing the subject. And then he kissed her forehead softly. "Survived long enough to discover something pretty precious."

"I wish I could go with you tomorrow," she said. "Will you be gone very long?" Suddenly, even a few hours was too long a time for them to be separated.

He nodded. "I'm afraid so. Besides putting Meredith on the plane, I've got to talk to the man at the government office. . . ."

He let his voice trail off mysteriously. Chyna knit her brows together, waiting. "Why?" she finally asked.

"I need to extend the work permit," he told her. "We've lost two days. Or haven't you noticed?"

"You don't intend to make them up?" she asked, wondering if he were just pretending for her benefit, and hating being plagued by these doubts.

"Yes," he answered. "With two more days." For a moment the atmosphere became serious. "Does that answer your question?" he asked, looking at her intently.

"Yes," she said quietly. "That answers my question. And you'll talk to Dussault before you go?" she asked, still not able to believe totally that what she had hoped for in her heart was really true.

"And I'll talk to Dussault before I go," he said, parroting her words in a singsong fashion. "But right now I've had enough of words," he told her.

She saw the gleam that came into his eyes. "You're kidding," she murmured.

He shook his head. "Abstinence builds up strength," he told her.

"It certainly must," she whispered against his mouth just before he kissed her again.

But he didn't talk to Dussault before he left.

Chyna tried to keep her bitter disappointment from eating away at her. He was just in a hurry, she tried to tell herself. They had overslept, and he'd had only an hour and a half to get Meredith to the airport. He had tried to talk to the director, she reminded herself, but for once the man was nowhere to be found. Someone finally told Matt that Dussault was scouting another location with the cinematographer.

So much for words of caution, Chyna thought with a touch of fear. As she watched Matt and the others driving away, she could feel herself growing uneasy. She tried to tell herself that she was just being superstitious.

Chyna turned her attention back to the stunt coordinator, who was telling her what he wanted her to do during the fight scene. Sally stood at Alex's elbow, wearing a torn white dress. Chyna looked like a carbon copy of the actress, her hair disarrayed in the same manner, her dress torn in the same places. Both women had been carefully scrutinized by the makeup, wardrobe and continuity people for exactness of detail.

Dussault marched over to join them. Chyna quickly masked the involuntary frown that sprang to her lips. "Are you ready for a take?" he barked. Before Chyna or the other stuntworker had a chance to answer, Dussault was waving the cameras onto the scene.

The positioning of the cameras was all-important for a fight scene. Chyna knew that she had to keep her back to the camera at all times. That way, the swing she took at the "villain" could miss by a country mile and still look effective on screen. It pleased Chyna to double for a feisty heroine. It also pleased her pocket. If the heroine hadn't been in danger all the time, Chyna's paycheck would have reflected that fact. She had arranged to be paid by the stunt rather than the customary five hundred dollars a day that many of the stuntworkers earned. So far, the total was adding up quite nicely.

"Okay, let's do it!" Dussault roared. After the appropriate commands the camera directly behind Chyna dollied in for a close-up of Sally.

"Cut!" Dussault commanded, and Sally willingly stepped away to let Chyna move in.

"Roll 'em!"

With that the fight was on. All Chyna was supposed to do was take a good swing at the villain who was running toward her, appearing to hit his midsection with the butt of a rifle. She checked her swing just in time, and the stuntman fell at her feet, doubled over, an appropriately dazed look on his face.

"Cut!"

She wasn't sure, but Dussault didn't sound very pleased. And he wasn't.

"I want you to come in closer when you swing," Dussault snapped at Chyna.

Was he crazy? "Any closer and I'll hit him," she protested, glancing at the stuntman, who was brushing

165

himself off. He looked none too happy about the director's orders. "The camera—"

"I'll take care of the camera," Dussault told her coldly. "You just take orders. I want you to come in closer this time."

Chyna and the stuntman exchanged looks, then prepared to do it again. Chyna could feel the tension mounting.

Four takes went by before Dussault finally muttered something about that being good enough. He went on to another part of the scene, leaving Chyna free to rehearse her next stunt. This time, another stuntman was to come running from behind and tackle her, making her fall and roll in the dirt. It didn't seem very difficult, Chyna thought as the two of them began to practice.

She had taken exactly three falls before she noticed that the cameras were being set up nearby. She looked up, watching as Dussault began to browbeat the head cameraman.

This has the makings of a long, long day, she thought, getting up.

"Don't we get any more time to practice?" she asked Alex. "It's still a little rough."

"You should have had the kinks out by now," Dussault retorted, overhearing her. "We're already two days behind. We're going to make them up. That means I don't have time to coddle nervous stunt-men."

"Matt said he was getting a work permit extension—" Chyna began. But her words were cut short by the look Dussault gave her. He seemed to be telling her not to be so gullible. Chyna pressed her lips together and fell silent, wishing she could be certain that Matt had been telling the truth. After all, the words would have been easy enough to say. And she wasn't going to see him actually apply for the extension. It would be easy enough for him to say that the extension had been denied for some reason or other.

"That's a nasty one," the makeup artist was saying.

"Yes, he is," Chyna muttered.

"No, I mean your bruise," the man pointed out, applying the appropriate shade of body makeup to the point of her shoulder where the dress was torn. It felt a little tender as his fingers brushed against it, and Chyna winced.

"I guess we're all just so anxious to please," she mumbled, "that we get carried away."

"I wish someone would carry him away," the makeup man said under his breath.

"You're not the only one," Chyna told him.

"Let's go, let's go!" Dussault yelled.

"Showtime," Chyna sighed, stepping back before the camera.

They broke for lunch right after the shot had been successfully completed. Dussault limited the break to half an hour, and told everyone to turn up for the fire sequence next. After she grabbed a sandwich, Chyna had only enough time left to change her costume.

At least this time she had pants on, she thought. The dresses worn by the heroine hampered her movements, and she still harbored bad memories of the time when she had caught on fire. She felt she had more of a sporting chance in pants. And the way Dussault was going, she was going to need all the help she could get. As she buttoned her blouse she wondered if Dussault was taking advantage of the fact that

Matt had gone into the city. Or wouldn't it have mattered?

Chyna sighed. She had to put these doubts out of her head for the time being. She needed to concentrate on her gag.

"You ready?" she asked Pepper.

She glanced at her friend and saw that the woman looked uncharacteristically nervous.

"You okay?" she asked when Pepper made no answer.

Quickly a smile flashed across Pepper's face. "Sure, just thinking," she said as she walked out the door.

"About what?" Chyna prodded as she followed her out.

"About another profession." Pepper laughed. "God, that Dussault is a hell-raiser, isn't he?"

"I was thinking that hell was more where he belonged," Chyna quipped.

When they got to where the huge tent was set up, Chyna was surprised to see some of the special effects people getting ready to set fire to it. "I didn't know they were going to shoot the fire today."

Pepper merely shrugged in response. "Who knows what he has in mind?"

"Hey, you two, over here!" Dussault ordered, waving them over to the tight circle that had gathered around him.

Dubiously Chyna led the way, wondering what the director was up to.

"I want you all inside," he said once the two women were within earshot. "We're going ahead with the fire scene. I've got the cameras all set up. If we do it right, we can get this shot in one take. Then we won't have to face the expense of burning two tents."

Chyna's mouth dropped open. What about the possible expenditure of lives? She looked at the startled faces around her. Wasn't anyone going to say anything? But she knew better. Protests didn't endear you to the men who made movies. Damn it, where was Matt when she needed him?

But would it matter if he were here?

"Okay, you, you and you," Dussault said, pointing to Chyna and two of the stuntmen as he consulted his storyboard for positions. "I want you—"

"No," Chyna said, not budging.

The other two stuntmen stopped walking, not daring to side with her, yet curious as to what was going to happen next.

Dussault's shaggy brows formed one straight, angry line. "No?" he echoed, surprised. "Did I hear you right?"

Chyna looked toward Alex for support. But the stunt coordinator didn't make a sound. He was watching warily. "We're not ready to film this," she said, measuring her words carefully.

She could see the color rising to Dussault's cheeks. "I say when you're ready to do something!" he informed her, barely suppressed rage in his words. "What is it? Aren't you brave enough to try it?" he taunted.

"No," she said, trying to keep her voice calm. "Just not stupid enough."

"Look," he said, jabbing a finger at her, "just because Harrigan wasted a little time on you and you did some tricks for his kid doesn't make you something special. You have no say in the matter—"

"Matt said—"

"The only thing Harrigan cares about is getting this

picture done on time. His reputation is riding on it. One colossal money-eater could be a death warrant for his career."

She knew that what he was saying was true. In the movie business nobody cared about your past accomplishments. It was what you had done lately that counted with the studios. Failure took on much larger proportions than success did.

"I thought he was keeping you in line," Dussault snapped. "Obviously his methods don't work very well."

His words stung her, and she didn't hear what he said next. Just when she had been beginning to believe that Matt really did care for her . . . Had she been right all along? Had he been playing up to her just to keep her quiet?

"Now, you do this scene, or you never do another scene as long as you live!" Dussault threatened. She knew he could make good on his threat. He was important—and vindictive—enough to do just that.

Common sense told her to walk away from the set. What he was asking them to do would be dangerous enough even with adequate rehearsal. Without that rehearsal, Dussault was pushing for orchestrated suicide. But somehow that didn't matter to her right then. Matt's behavior toward her had been a game after all. And she had been a king-sized dupe.

"Well?" Dussault demanded impatiently, his hands on his hips.

"All right," she said hollowly. "I'll do your damn scene."

As she walked inside the huge tent, she heard Dussault laughing to someone. "They always come around when it means money."

12

With raw determination, Chyna began to execute her stunt, which involved making her way along the inside wall of the huge tent and then actually rolling through the flames as she grappled with two assailants. She kept her eye on the flames at all times. When you were dealing with fire, you had to have a healthy respect for your co-star. It demanded your attention.

She wasn't exactly sure when or how it happened, but suddenly her co-star took over center stage. Whipping her head around, Chyna saw flames devouring their way to the top of the tent.

This wasn't in the script!

"Film it, damn you. Film it! This will look terrific!" she heard Dussault yell above the roar of the fire.

"My God, it's going out of control!" Pepper shouted, staring up as she backed away from the center of the tent. Everyone began scrambling for safety.

"Where are the fire extinguishers?" Chyna cried as she grabbed Alex's hand.

"Over there!" he shouted back as the noise grew louder. He pointed off to the right side of the tent, where several men were vainly attempting to douse the fire, which was spreading.

"But there should be more!" she insisted, scanning the area. It was hard to focus on anything as panic spread through the crew and smoke filled the air.

Alex pulled her back as a piece of the tent suddenly fell down in front of them, still blazing. "He's got them at the other location!"

He pushed her outside as the props and equipment that had been set up for the scene began to catch fire. They would be standing in an inferno in a matter of minutes if something wasn't done.

"Move the Jeeps," Alex roared, waving at the others, "before the gas tanks explode!"

Several stuntmen dashed toward the cars, and seconds later the sound of engines being gunned added to the general mayhem. The scene was a tangle of cables, equipment and fleeing people.

"Alex!" Chyna cried, pointing to the tent. The flames were searing through the top. They had to get the tent down so they could extinguish the fire before it spread to the surrounding vegetation.

"Way ahead of you." He nodded. "Find something sharp. Use anything you can, but start cutting that tent down! I'm going back inside to get that center pole down," he called. "I'll be back in two minutes."

"Pull up the stakes!" Chyna cried to one of the stuntmen. An extra ran by and she pulled his sword from the scabbard dangling at his side.

It wasn't very sharp, and she muttered an oath as

she hacked at the strong cord that attached the tent to the stake. After several desperate tries, she finally severed the rope, and the edge of the tent sprang free and collapsed toward the center. But the main support for the tent was still standing, and that meant Alex was still inside!

Dussault was standing nearby, frozen. He was staring in disbelief at the fire, oblivious to all the turmoil and noise around him. He looked horror stricken.

But she had no time to think about him. "Alex is still in there!" she cried to someone at her elbow. She turned and recognized Scottie. "We've got to get him out of there!"

This was just another gag, she told herself over and over again as she reentered the inferno. Just another gag. She held her frayed nerves together. There was no time for fear now. Later she could fall apart.

Smoke and fire were everywhere within the tent. It was far more devastating than anything that could be captured on film. Chyna's eyes swept the interior, looking for Alex. Scottie had followed her in, and now tugged at her sleeve and pointed overhead. Shielding her eyes, Chyna could just barely make out the figure of a man climbing up to the top of the center pole. When he reached the top, Alex began to frantically hack away at the rigging.

"Alex, get down from there!" Chyna shrieked.

If he heard her, he gave no indication, working at the ropes until one line finally tore free. The second, third and fourth followed suit in quick succession. That job done, Alex began to slide down the pole as the walls of the tent collapsed around him. He apparently didn't realize that the bottom five feet of the pole were

173

engulfed in flames. Chyna stripped off her jacket and began beating at the fire, trying to keep the pole from collapsing until Alex made it down. Scottie joined in, but it was no use. Chyna heard a horrible crack and the pole began to go, severed by the fire. Alex leaped down, twisting his leg beneath him in the fall.

Chyna and Scottie rushed to him and each grabbed an arm to drag him away from burning canvas as it fell. When they got outside the area was swarming with more grips, who had come running with fire extinguishers. A cheer of relief went up as the threesome joined the bedraggled extras and crew members.

"He needs medical attention," Chyna told Dussault, who, though no longer frozen, still looked pale and shaken. He nodded and turned to the two nearest men. "Get him to the first aid station." He sighed, his breath rattling in his chest. "Okay, everybody get cleaned up. The excitement's over."

"Not by a long shot," Chyna declared, her voice stone cold. The fire in her eyes rivaled the blaze. All she could think of was that he had almost killed them all.

Dussault turned to look at her, stunned. "What's the matter?" He tried to regain his former verve, but it was obvious that he was shaken to the core.

"We're not working anymore. Not until you're taken off the picture," Chyna said defiantly, suppressing her rage. He had nearly gotten them all killed, and all he could say was that the "excitement" was over. She felt hysteria mounting within her and fought to keep it under control.

"What do you mean?"

"If you hadn't been pushing, if you had left us with

enough time to rehearse this scene properly, if you hadn't had half the grips out working on another scene, then this wouldn't have happened." She gestured at the charred, smoldering remnants of the tent. "That makes you responsible! And no paycheck in the world is worth dying for." Her eyes narrowed. "I've got a lot of years ahead of me. I don't intend to let you make me lose them."

Dussault stared at her, knowing he had to do something to try to maintain control. He could see by the looks of the people around her that they agreed with her. "You're calling a strike!" he cried, licking his lips nervously. "You can't do that!"

"Call it what you like," Chyna said, rubbing away perspiration streaks with the back of her blackened hand. "It boils down to the fact that we won't work on an unsafe picture." The circle around her tightened, and Chyna knew that the others supported her. Finally. The hysteria within her abated a little.

"Do you realize what you're doing?" Dussault cried desperately. "You're jeopardizing Harrigan's picture!"

He was trying to get at her the only way he knew how, and for a moment uncertainty clawed at the pit of her stomach. What would Matt say when he found out what she had done? Would he feel betrayed by the woman he loved—or just furious that his attempt to control her had failed? But he wasn't there, and something had to be done until he got back. Dussault looked chastised, but how long would that last? No, Chyna felt that none of them could risk taking a chance. The next time might be fatal.

"No," she said softly. *"You're* jeopardizing Harrigan's picture," she said, turning away.

She was followed by the others, leaving Dussault to stare after them incredulously.

Matt returned an hour later, and he had been inside his trailer for exactly three minutes when the door burst open and Dussault stormed in, furious.

"She's done it, Matt. She's done it just like I warned you!"

"Sit down, Phil; you're turning red," Matt said calmly. He was tired from his trip, and in no mood for another outburst from Dussault. Although this time, he thought, looking closer at the man, he really looked strained. Matt moved toward the bar and began to pour himself a drink. He felt he was going to need it.

The scotch didn't prepare him in the slightest.

"She's called a strike," Dussault said, his voice trembling. He had never had his authority usurped before.

Matt's fingers tightened around his glass. "She's what?" His mind refused to register Dussault's words.

The director took the glass from Matt's hand, his own hand shaking as he took a long drink. "You heard me. She's called a strike."

"Chyna wouldn't do that," Matt said, his voice deadly still.

"Oh, wouldn't she?" Dussault asked, taking a second gulp.

"Why?" Matt demanded, numb. Had he been wrong about her all this time? Had he allowed his emotions to cloud his judgment?

"What does it matter why? She stood there in front of everyone and declared that they were calling a strike. She's got to go, Matt!" His bravado faded in light of the look in Matt's eyes. Dussault lowered his voice. "There was a fire. It got out of control. You know how those things can be."

He almost sounded as if he were pleading, Matt thought. It was totally out of character for the man. Tension formed in the pit of his stomach.

"You can't predict which way the wind goes, you know that," Dussault went on, rambling. He closed his eyes for a moment, trying to pull himself together. "She flew off the handle," the director continued, beginning to pace. "I warned you, Matt. I warned you," he repeated. "She's costing you money every minute we're in here talking."

"We're not in here talking," Matt corrected. "You are. I'm listening." *And hating what I hear.* "And I—"

He didn't get a chance to finish, for the door swung open again, banging against the opposite wall.

"Want to hear my side of it?" Chyna asked, afraid of what Dussault might have told him. What lies was she going to be up against? Dussault looked desperate. He'd say anything to downplay his part in the disaster.

Matt had never seen her so angry. She was still in her bedraggled costume, and she smelled of smoke. "Are you all right?" he asked, moving toward her.

Chyna nodded. "No thanks to him." All her previous doubts about their relationship came to a head as she turned to look at Matt. This would be the telling moment. What if Dussault had been right?

"We'll go over budget if—" Dussault began hurriedly.

"Chyna was talking," Matt said quietly, cutting the other man off.

Chyna couldn't read the expression on Matt's face. Undoubtedly Dussault had said that she had called a strike. A strike on *Matt's* set. Would that make him prejudiced against anything she had to say in her own defense? She turned squarely to face him.

"He tried to film two sequences today. We didn't have enough time to rehearse all the segments that went into the fire scene, but he went ahead with it anyway. There weren't enough special effects grips to control the fire. Suddenly it was everywhere." An involuntary shudder ran through her. "It was Alex who cut the tent down. If he hadn't, an awful lot of people could have gotten hurt. Instead, only Alex did. He broke his leg." She glared accusingly at Dussault who, in turn, looked at Matt.

"These things happen, Matt," he insisted. "You know that. It's not my fault," he declared adamantly.

"They don't *have* to happen if you take the proper precautions!" Chyna cried. She felt herself on shaky ground, but she couldn't stop. To back down now would be selling out her integrity. But was she giving up Matt's love instead? She tried to force the question out of her mind. Matt had to understand. He just *had* to.

Dussault struggled for control. "Matt, we can have another crew out here in twenty-four hours if this is the way they want to play it," he said, his brown eyes shifting wildly as he searched Matt's face for some sign as to whose side he was on. But Matt's face remained grim.

Chyna had no clue, either, and she wished that things hadn't come to a head this way. But she couldn't stand by and let Dussault go on doing what he was doing. Someone had to try to stop him. Someone had to go on record against him. Sure, he had looked stricken out there as they carried Alex away, but how long would that last? Chyna knew she couldn't live with herself if she turned a blind eye to the events that had just transpired. It would be tantamount to condoning Dussault's behavior.

The specter of Neil's accident hung over her, and she knew that the stand she had taken was the only one open to her. Otherwise she would be haunted for the rest of her life.

Matt looked from one to the other, knowing that his next words might forever change his life in one way or another. Studios didn't like rebels, even rebel producers. He couldn't just fire a known talent like Dussault. But if he gave Chyna an ultimatum, telling her to return to work or else, he knew he would lose her. He couldn't afford to do either.

As he attempted to come up with a compromise, there was a knock on the door. Relieved at the distraction, he called out, "Come in."

Alex, his arm draped around Scottie's shoulders, hobbled in, pain etched into his dark features.

"What the hell are you doing here?" Matt demanded, striding over to him. "I'll get someone to drive you to the city—" he began, looking at the makeshift splint that had been put on the man's leg.

Alex nodded, an unreadable expression on his face. "I'd appreciate that, but first I have to talk to you."

Matt's expression darkened. "If you're going to tell me about the fire, Chyna already took care of that," he said, giving her an enigmatic look.

"No, I don't think she did," Alex said. Chyna looked at him sharply. There was something about his tone that bothered her. "Not all of it." He shifted a little, and Scottie struggled to keep him upright.

"Stop playing martyr in my trailer, Alex," Matt said,

his tone softening. "At least sit down." He tried to guide Alex to the sofa, but the stunt coordinator surprised him by waving him away.

"This isn't going to take long," he said, his voice devoid of expression. "The fire was my fault."

"What?" Chyna cried, stunned.

Alex looked at her, agony on his face. "It was my fault," he repeated.

"But how? . . . I don't . . ." Words failed her. Matt saw the utter confusion on her face and could only guess at what was going on inside.

"I came in here because I was afraid that Chyna would get fired. She stood up for us, for the whole crew," he clarified, "when she thought that the accident was Dussault's fault. But it wasn't." He measured his words carefully, even though they came out in a rush. It was, Chyna thought, as if he were trying to cleanse himself. "The assistant director was nervous about the shot. He asked me to cue the grips when to light the fire." He paused, licking his lips. "I miscalculated. I was premature. It was my fault."

The words had sounded hollow, but they rang over and over again in Chyna's ears. It was as if she had suddenly seen a ghost. She had been so concerned about safety, so concerned about the director taking precautions, that she had totally forgotten about the human factor. Numbed, Chyna sank down into a chair, unable to do anything except sit and watch Matt. What would he think of her?

His first concern was for Alex. "Scottie, get him into town and stay with him until they release him from the hospital. Take a driver with you." Alex and Matt exchanged a long look. "We'll talk about this later, Alex," Matt promised, his voice full of understanding sympathy. Alex's burden would be great enough without his adding any words to it now.

"As for our problem . . ." Matt began, turning back to Dussault and Chyna as the other two men left.

"There is no problem," Chyna said softly. She felt as if she were in a trance. She was only half-conscious of the fact that she had risen to her feet. "I'll save you the trouble of firing me," she told Matt. She turned to look at Dussault, who was still digesting what had just transpired. "I was wrong. I'm sorry. Something came over me. I guess I was still living with my husband's ghost." She took a deep breath. "I'll apologize to you in front of everyone before I leave if it will make a difference."

Before Dussault could answer, Matt cut in. "You're not going anywhere," he informed her. "We're not finished shooting here."

"But I—"

"Woman, would you please stop talking for once? You're one of the best stuntworkers in the business. I know that. Dussault knows that." He cast a meaningful glance at the director. The man forced himself to nod his agreement. "What happened here today should have taught us *all* a lesson. Maybe different lessons," he added, for Chyna's benefit. "But I'm not about to let hot tempers disrupt my set. *I* say who goes and who stays. And I haven't fired anyone." He fished a long thin envelope out of his hip pocket and threw it on the desk in front of him. "That's our extension. We have an extra week if we need it. No reason to hurry any longer. Studio money isn't everything. Once this picture is released, it'll earn back what was laid out here in a couple of weeks. I guarantee it. And I know my movies," he said firmly. "Now, get out of here, both of you," he said wearily, turning his back on them. "Tomorrow we'll all start fresh."

Dussault was quick to take his leave, but Chyna remained where she was, looking at Matt's back. Fear and uncertainty gnawed at her, feelings that were far greater than anything she had felt during the fire. Drawing on her last shred of courage, she reached out and touched his shoulder. "Matt, I—"

Matt turned around. His eyes appraised her for a long moment before he said anything. "Why couldn't you have waited until I got back before making that grandstand play?"

His words stung her. But he was right. Still, she wanted him to understand. "The accident brought everything back to me. I . . . I overreacted." She swallowed, trying to get rid of the scratchy feeling in her throat. She looked up toward the ceiling, hoping to keep her tears back. "I lost my head. I—" Abruptly she stopped, overwhelmed by the enormity of the situation.

Despite his own anger, Matt understood what she was going through, and he drew her into his arms. Nothing mattered right then, just as long as she was safe.

Chyna sagged against him, momentarily drained. "Oh, Matt, I was wrong, so wrong. All this time . . ." She sighed deeply. "It's like a rock's been lifted off my chest." She looked up into his face, "Can you forgive me?" The tears spilled out freely now, making tracks through the soot on her face.

He took out his handkerchief and wiped some of the dirt away. "I'll think about it," he said, a hint of warmth in his voice. "This is getting to be a habit," he commented, nodding toward his handkerchief.

"Poor Alex," Chyna murmured.

"I'll talk to him when he gets back. I'll talk to a lot of people," he added. "There should have been a way to prevent this."

"But Alex said—"

"I know what Alex said, but there should have been someone double-checking both of them. I'm not whitewashing Phil just because I didn't have him taken off the picture. He was wrong in rushing production. And I was wrong in not taking a stronger stand with him. And you," he said, touching her nose, "were wrong for putting me on the spot. Now we'll all do penance and be better for it."

He pressed her against him, stroking her hair. "I'll file a report when we get back," he promised.

"You'd do that for me?" she asked, knowing what such an action could mean as far as the studio was concerned.

"No," he said slowly, "I'll do it for me. You don't have a private patent on integrity, you know."

She couldn't believe it. "Do you really feel that way?"

"Would I lie to you?" he asked, searching her face for a sign of trust. She was so hard to read at times, so complex, so intense, yet gentle. What had life been like without her? Empty, he thought. Very, very empty.

"I don't know," she said honestly. "Why not? *I* lie to me. I spent all afternoon telling myself I didn't care about you. . . ."

"And you were lying?" he asked softly.

"Viciously." Chyna kissed him soundly, lacking any other way to express her feelings of overwhelming gratitude.

Halfway through the kiss, Matt began to cough. "God, you smell awful."

"You would too if you just came out of a burning inferno," she informed him, a warm feeling beginning to spread all through her.

"Do you stuntpeople play with fire often?"

"Sometimes when we don't even know it," she said, running her hand along his shirt. She began to open the buttons.

"Well, you'll just have to take a shower before you come home every night. I like your natural smell much better—before you're hickory smoked."

Chyna stopped pulling out his shirttails. "Are you asking me to move in with you?"

"In a manner of speaking, yes." He urged her hand back into motion.

"But what will Wanda say?" she asked. His words had thrown her completely off balance. A glimmer of hope began to sparkle.

"Probably 'Good afternoon, Mrs. Harrigan.'"

She stared at him. "You're asking me to marry you?" Oh please, please say you're asking me to marry you.

"No," he quipped, "just to change your name. The space on the mailbox can't accommodate two names." He swept her closer into his arms, laughing. "Of course I'm asking you to marry me."

"But I just started a strike on your picture. I don't—" Confusion reigned supreme in her brain as logic and emotions ran into each other. He wanted to marry her. Nothing else in the world mattered. Stop trying to talk him out of it, dummy, she told herself. He loves you!

"And we've resolved that," he said, kissing her cheek. "What's the problem?"

"Nothing," Chyna laughed, feeling giddy. "Nothing at all."

"Glad to hear it," he answered. "Did you know I was superstitious?" he asked her suddenly.

"You?" The idea seemed impossible. He was far too logical a person to hold with any superstitions, she thought.

He nodded, then paused to kiss the outer rim of her ear. A shiver slid down her spine. "Come here," he said, leading her to the couch. He gently sat her down and then began to work on her boots, pulling off one and then the other while he spoke. "I'm beginning to feel as if I need a good luck talisman to ward off any further problems on the set."

"A talisman?" Chyna echoed.

"Right. In the olden days ladies would send their knights off to battle wearing a scarf or something to act as a talisman. Got anything for me?" he asked. As he spoke, he was unhooking her trousers.

"How about a blouse?" she offered mischievously.

He slipped it off her shoulders and examined it. "Nope," he decided, tossing it aside.

"Trousers?"

They came off too. "Sorry, too dull looking," he told her, letting them join her blouse on the floor.

"Bra?"

"Worth considering," he agreed, taking it from her and rubbing the soft, lacy material against his cheek. She felt warmed by the glow in his eyes as he looked at her.

"Almost," he said, then sighed. "But not quite."

"Well," she said playfully, "all I've got left are my panties."

He snapped his fingers. "That just might do the trick." With that he eased the translucent blue material away from her body. "Yes," he whispered, not looking at the prize in his hand, only at her. "That just might do the trick."

He moved to cover her body with his own, unable to put up with the separation any longer.

"You're going to look pretty silly walking around the set with blue panties tied around your arm," she murmured against his lips.

"I'll chance it," he told her, beginning to explore her body. "After all, I'm the guy who took a chance on having a hell-raiser as part of my crew, remember?"

Wonderful sensations began to unfold all through her as anticipation took hold. "I remember," she said softly. "Matt?"

"Hmm?" The sound rippled against her taut belly, making it quiver. Matt raised his head. "You're interrupting my concentration."

"Do you love me?"

"You picked a strange time to ask," he said, pulling himself back up to look into her face.

"On the contrary, I think it's a very opportune time," she pointed out teasingly. "Do you?" She needed to hear him say it almost as much as she needed to feel his body against hers.

"Lady," he said, gently brushing the hair away from her face, "you've been walking through the shadows of my mind ever since I first laid eyes on you." Ever so tenderly, he kissed first one eyelid and then the other. "I don't think I'd really want to go on living if I couldn't have you. And in my book, Ms. Daredevil, that means

I love you very, very much." He kissed her lips lightly. "Satisfied?"

"No," she answered, entwining her fingers through the hair at the nape of his neck. "But I think you'll see to that shortly."

The laughter in his eyes faded into passion. "You bet I will. Want to come back here on our honeymoon?" he asked.

"Not on your life!" she murmured feelingly, just before she brought his mouth down on hers and stopped saying anything at all.

Silhouette Desire

SEPTEMBER TITLES

CATTLEMAN'S CHOICE
Diana Palmer

HUNGRY FOR LOVE
Ariel Berk

JOURNEY TO DESIRE
Laurie Paige

A DIFFERENT REALITY
Nora Powers

A WOMAN OF INTEGRITY
Marie Nicole

GOLDEN MAN
Ann Major

SEPTEMBER TITLES

DAZZLE
Ann Major

SARAH'S CHILD
Linda Howard

STOLEN THUNDER
Natalie Bishop

INTRIGUE IN VENICE
Tracy Sinclair

A DANGEROUS PRECEDENT
Lisa Jackson

AN ACQUIRED TASTE
Kathryn Thiels

Four New
Silhouette Romances
could be yours
ABSOLUTELY FREE

Did you know that Silhouette Romances are no longer available from the shops in the U.K?

Read on to discover how you could receive four brand new Silhouette Romances, **free** and **without obligation,** with this special introductory offer to the new Silhouette Reader Service.

As thousands of women who have read these books know — Silhouette Romances sweep you away into an exciting love filled world of fascination between men and women. A world filled with

age-old conflicts — love and money, ambition and guilt, jealousy and pride, even life and death.

Silhouette Romances are the latest stories written by the world's best romance writers, and they are **only** available from Silhouette Reader Service. Take out a subscription and you could receive 6 brand new titles every month, plus a newsletter bringing you all the latest information from Silhouette's New York editors. All this delivered in one exciting parcel direct to your door, with no charges for postage and packing.

And at only 95p for a book, Silhouette Romances represent the very best value in Romantic Reading.

Remember, Silhouette Romances are **only** available to subscribers, so don't miss out on this very special opportunity. Fill in the certificate below and post it today. You don't even need a stamp.

--- --- --- --- --- --- --- --- --- --- --- --- --- --- ✂ --- ---

FREE BOOK CERTIFICATE

To: Silhouette Reader Service, FREEPOST, P.O. Box 236, Croydon, Surrey. CR9 9EL

Readers in South Africa—write to:
Silhouette Romance Club, Private Bag X3010, Randburg 2125.

Yes, please send me, free and without obligation, four brand new Silhouette Romances and reserve a subscription for me. If I decide to subscribe, I shall receive six brand new books every month for £5.70 , post and packing free. If I decide not to subscribe I shall write to you within 10 days. The free books are mine to keep, whatever I decide. I understand that I may cancel my subscription at any time simply by writing to you. I am over 18 years of age. Please write in BLOCK CAPITALS.

Signature _____

Name _____

Address _____

_____ Postcode _____

SEND NO MONEY — TAKE NO RISKS.
Please don't forget to include your Postcode.

Remember postcodes speed delivery Offer applies in U K only and is not valid to present subscribers Silhouette reserve the right to exercise discretion in granting membership If price changes are necessary you will be notified. Offer expires December 1985.

EPS1

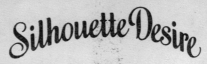

Silhouette Desire

Your chance to write back!

We'll send you details of an exciting free offer from *SILHOUETTE*, if you can help us by answering the few simple questions below.

Just fill in this questionnaire, tear it out and put it in an envelope and post today to: Silhouette Reader Survey, FREEPOST, P.O. Box 236, Croydon, Surrey CR9 9EL. You don't even need a stamp.

What is the title of the *SILHOUETTE Desire* you have just read?

_____

How much did you enjoy it?

Very much ☐   Quite a lot ☐   Not very much ☐

Would you buy another *SILHOUETTE Desire* book?

Yes ☐   Possibly ☐   No ☐

How did you discover *SILHOUETTE Desire* books?

Advertising ☐   A friend ☐   Seeing them on sale ☐

Elsewhere (please state) _____

How often do you read romantic fiction?

Frequently ☐   Occasionally ☐   Rarely ☐

Name (Mrs/Miss) _____

Address _____

_____

_____ **Postcode** _____

Age group: Under 24 ☐   25–34 ☐   35–44 ☐

45–55 ☐   Over 55 ☐

Silhouette Reader Service, P.O. Box 236, Croydon, Surrey CR9 9EL.
Readers in South Africa—write to:
Silhouette Romance Club,
Private Bag X3010, Randburg 2125.

SD1